Taxi F‹

"If you like your mystery with a paranormal edge, then you should be reading this series." ~Cheryl Green

Praise for Renaissance Faire Mysteries

"**Fatal Fairies** was a good read. I loved being back at the Renaissance Faire Village with Jessie, Chase and all of the village characters. I like the magical twist that happens to Jessie in this book and I'm curious to see what other magic happens in future books. Thank you Joyce and Jim for writing a great story that transported me to a village I wouldn't mind living in! Eagerly awaiting the next book in the series!" ~ **R. Davila**

Praise for Missing Pieces Mysteries

"I really enjoyed **A Watery Death**, it was full of a few surprises and a very nice guest appearance that was fun to read about. As well as a nice surprise but sad guest appearance to enjoy. Can't wait for the next book!" ~ **April Schilling**

Praise for the Retired Witches Mysteries

"**Spell Booked** kept me guessing. Who was good, who could be trusted, and who was the rogue witch? Joyce and James Lavene created a world where magic and mundane live together yet separate-even in the same households." ~ **Cozy Up With Kathy**

Some of our other series:

Renaissance Faire Mysteries
Wicked Weaves
Ghastly Glass
Deadly Daggers
Harrowing Hats
Treacherous Toy
Perilous Pranks — Novella
Murderous Matrimony
Bewitching Boots

Missing Pieces Mysteries
A Timely Vision
A Touch of Gold
A Spirited Gift
A Haunting Dream
A Finder's Fee
Dae's Christmas Past
A Watery Death

Taxi for the Dead Mysteries
Undead by Morning
Broken Hearted Ghoul
Dead Girl Blues

Retired Witches Mysteries
Spell Booked
Looking for Mr. Good Witch

A Dickens of a Murder

A Canterville Book Shop Mystery

By

Joyce and Jim Lavene

Acknowledgments:
The authors want to acknowledge three readers for their help in choosing names for the pets in this book: Melissa La Pierre, for Truffles, in memory; Erika Kehlet for Puck; Noelle Marie for Wordsworth; and Linda Rima for Maggie May.
All chapter quotes are attributable to Charles Dickens.

Dedication:
This book is in memory of Joyce Lavene who passed away on October 20, 2015
We will miss her and hope her memory and works live on as she would want them to.

Chapter One

The Corpse

"Marley was dead to begin with, this must be distinctly understood, or nothing wonderful can come of the story I am going to relate."

It was two weeks until Thanksgiving. There were already wreaths and lights on almost every house in Olde Town, Portsmouth, Virginia. A light fall of crisp, white frost was still hard on the lawns where angels and Santas waited for the big day. The stores were bustling with shoppers, and pumpkin spice coffee had been available at the local coffee shop for a week.

Simon and I stared at the high roof of the three-story Victorian home. The morning sun glinted off the new, green shingles on the impressive front turret — right beside the man lying upside down on the roof.

"How long do you think he's been up there?"

He was almost in the position of the Hanged Man of the Tarot — one knee bent, the other leg straight behind him. His face was turned away from us, to the right, so we couldn't tell who he was. He was simply dangling there, as though suspended by an unseen thread.

Simon Canterville shook his graying, shoulder-length locks. He was taller than the average man of a certain age, and his body was straight and narrow like an old plank. He wore his usual conservative, black, Victorian-style suit with dignity. It might have looked comical on anyone else but one look into his clear, blue eyes would have ended that misconception. He was not a man to be trifled with, despite his eccentricities.

"You can never be certain what you're going to find these days when you look up, Miss Wellman. Best to call the police. They can deal with the burglar or whatever he may be." His voice still held the clipped remnants of his British homeland.

"He might be the cable installer," I suggested. "He wasn't supposed to be here until later today, but they aren't always right on time. I can't imagine why else anyone would be on the roof."

"Cable, eh?" Simon nodded. "I once worked on a vessel laying transatlantic cable from here to my beloved England. Not a job for the faint of heart, you know."

"I'm sure it wasn't." I was already used to the

random tales of his life. They popped out of him at the least provocation. I didn't mind. Simon had traveled the world and had fascinating stories to tell, like the books I loved so much.

I had been acquainted with Simon for years. He'd come into the Portsmouth Public Library almost every day while I was a librarian there. We'd only been partners in a new venture—The Canterville Book Shop—for the last two weeks.

Having rarely done anything surprising or crazy in my entire life, it had been a delirious roller coaster.

A loose, dark lock escaped the confines of my ponytail holder. I tucked it in with a promise to capture it more permanently at the first opportunity. I was dark-haired like my mother and sisters, all of us named Elizabeth with various diminutives—Liz and Beth for my sisters, Lisa for me. My writing group had encouraged me to describe my brown eyes as 'inquisitive'. My mother had told me that the green flecks in their centers made me see the world in ways that others didn't.

Of medium height and build, I felt diminutive and chubby beside Simon with his long, thin legs. I had a tendency to gain weight rather than lose it during times of stress, probably because I enjoyed rather than avoided cookies during those moments.

"What's going on out here?" Mrs. Hermione Tappen was wearing her usual business suit, this time in mauve, with matching pumps and jangling gold bracelets. Her unnaturally blond hair was curled and coiffed so that it never dared move. A heavy application of makeup made it difficult to say if she was closer to fifty or sixty. "What are you looking at up there?"

"There is a man on the roof," Simon told her
bluntly. He had little time or patience for Mrs. Tappen,
calling her 'that real-estate woman' in a scornful tone. It
seemed she regularly and obnoxiously offered to sell
his house for him, despite the fact that he'd never asked
her to.

I hadn't known her long enough to know if he was
right. "We think he may be running the cable."

"The cable?" Mrs. Tappen squinted at the man on
the roof since she hadn't put in her contacts yet. "Don't
they run that underground?"

"I have no idea," Simon replied. "And I have work
to do, as do you, Miss Wellman. We can't gawk at the
man all day. Let him get on with his business."

A shiny, brown Ford pulled up to the curb beside
us. There was no siren running, but a light flashed
inside. A man in his mid-thirties with bright, auburn
hair got out and came around the car. His brown suit
was tailored to fit his broad shoulders, muscular back,
and chest. He wasn't of football-player dimensions but
clearly worked out. Large sunglasses covered his eyes
and hid some of the many freckles on his face.

Mrs. Tappen admired him from head to toe with a
small smile playing on her hastily rouged lips.

"Excuse me." The handsome man in the suit took
out a badge and notebook as he removed his dark
glasses. "I'm Deputy Chief Daniel Fairhaven. We got a
call that there's a dead man on a roof."

I gulped hard and felt my stomach drop to my toes
before it zoomed back up where it belonged again. I
could hardly believe my eyes. "Daniel?"

Without studying him, I knew that he had a nice

smile, though he tried to hide it to keep up his tough-cop appearance. He had good teeth as well, white and even. His eyes were a warm, tender blue when he drank wine—and when he made love. They were cool when he was unhappy.

He was also my ex-husband.

"Lisa." He curtly nodded, barely glancing at me even though he hadn't seen me in years. I knew him well enough to know that he wasn't surprised to find me there. My well-honed, suspicious nature urged me forward into uncharted territory. "What are you doing here?"

"Dead body." He pointed at the roof and then at himself. "Cop."

"A dead man?" Simon glanced back at the roof. "Miss Wellman? Is the man on the roof dead?"

"I don't know," I answered quickly. "I didn't call the police."

Logic reasserted itself as the shock of seeing him wore off.

Something odd was up, or Daniel wouldn't have been there. Surely it was more than just a dead body, as terrible as that sounded. He'd done well for himself the last few years, following in his father's footsteps.

Daniel was Deputy Chief of Police, and wouldn't investigate homicides unless they involved an important or notorious death.

Exactly who was on the roof?

"I made the call." Admiral William Leazer, our neighbor on the left, spoke up. "Of course he's dead. No man's neck is naturally at that angle."

Admiral Leazer had been retired from the Navy for twenty years. He was a man with stern features, a broad chest, and narrow hips. His voice boomed as though he was still barking out orders to his recruits on a ship.

Daniel shook hands with the Admiral. "Thank you for your service, sir."

"Just doing what's right," the Admiral said gruffly. "Plain to see these people were going to hang around all day staring at him. Fairhaven, eh? Any relation to the past Chief of Police?"

"My father, sir."

"I see." Admiral Leazer snorted. "Huge shoes to fill there, son. My condolences."

Simon introduced himself to Daniel and told him that the three-story Victorian where the dead man was located belonged to him.

There wasn't time to ask questions as neighbors spilled out into the chilly morning, wanting to know what was wrong. Another police car arrived, this one marked with the city's logo. I watched Daniel as he shook hands and greeted people who questioned him. He didn't look at me again, and I tried not to stare at him.

But I was. Staring, that is.

I hadn't seen him in person since the terrible day we'd signed our divorce papers. That was so long ago—twelve years, to be exact. I'd seen him in newspapers and on TV, of course, but this was different. Up close, I could see that his youthful good looks had a more attractive, mature quality. He looked darn good though I hated to admit it.

We'd married in haste while we were in college, sneaking out late one night for the long drive to Myrtle Beach, giggling like little children, kissing like lovers when we had to stop at red lights. I'd been convinced that we loved each other deeply and passionately, despite our differences. What did those differences matter to a love like ours?

We'd come home and showed off our cheap rings to our angry parents, smiling smugly in the face of their disapproval. We hadn't cared. We'd been in love, and we were going to prove it to the world.

But it had turned out that they were right. We'd been going in two different directions and couldn't work out our differences. He'd always been on a fast-track to be police chief like his father. Or maybe to the mayor's office like his uncle. His sister was a junior District Attorney. Sheesh!

I had always seemed destined to work at the library. Books and reading were my passion. I had no ambitions to be head librarian. I just wanted to be there to breathe in the scent of books and handle them each day.

But that was a long time ago. Sometimes it seemed like someone else's life.

Now I watched him from the perspective of my own twelve years of maturity. I wished I had a coat to wrap around me instead of standing there in my oldest jeans and a green sweater. My hair was a mess, curls everywhere, and I wasn't wearing any makeup.

Not that I thought he'd notice. He was probably married by now and had children. There was no pain at that thought, just a faint interest in how my life could have been.

Several more people appeared, brought out of the nearby colorful Victorian houses by curiosity. Two more vehicles—one a police crime scene van and another a clearly marked police car—joined them.

By then it was established by an officer on the roof that, without a doubt, the man was dead.

Two crime scene techs in blue jumpsuits put ladders against the house and stormed the wall to examine the dead man as a firetruck also appeared.

"I'd like to get statements from everyone here," Daniel said. "May we use a room in the house, Mr. Canterville? It shouldn't take too long."

Simon imperiously lifted his chin.

I spoke quickly, knowing what his reply would be. "Of course. Please come inside." He was going to have to learn to let strangers into the house or the book shop would soon be dead as well.

Even though Simon wanted to open his old house to the public, he had an aversion to having strangers in his home. I'd seen the look on his face and knew he was about to decline an invitation to his neighbors as well as the police.

I didn't want him to appear suspicious even though the dead man was on his roof. Of course he was the first person the police would talk to. I'd learned enough about writing mysteries, and reading them, to know a suspect when I saw one.

It occurred to me that I could be under suspicion too. The dead man was right under my window in the third-floor turret room.

"Aptly said, Miss Wellman," Simon responded to my cue. "Of course. There must be a place to interview the suspects on the scene. When I briefly worked for Scotland Yard as a young man, the best information came from the kitchen or the parlor. Come in, ladies and gentlemen. Miss Wellman, please fetch tea."

"Thank you, Miss *Wellman*." Daniel managed a tight smile.

"You're welcome, Detective Fairhaven."

If he was upset that I wasn't using his name anymore, he'd just have to get over it. I'd taken back my maiden name almost as soon as the divorce papers were signed. Best to move on, my mother had said, and she'd been right.

We walked up the short flight of stairs to the beautiful wrap-around porch and antique door with a stained-glass window set in it. Simon had already replaced the window with the cardinal in it for one with an image of books. It was a nice touch.

"What are you doing here, Lisa?" Daniel asked as I opened the front door.

"I work here. We're setting up a book shop together. As you can see, there are more than enough books."

The door swung open into the elegant foyer with a large, crystal chandelier. Stacks of books were everywhere on shelves, embroidered chairs, and velvet sofas. Books filled most of the wide stairs going to the second floor and had replaced planters in windows with good light. Every flat surface was covered in books, even the old Victrola with my tortie cat, Truffles, on it.

The books were mostly fiction. Those were Simon's favorite. Mine too. We'd decided to add the few nonfiction titles to the rooms with similar fiction — the Teddy Roosevelt Room with historical fiction, the Ann McGaffrey Room with science fiction, and so forth. Brass plates were on each door to designate what books were within.

Simon and I shared a love of mysteries, although his tended to be older titles written primarily by men. I liked the newer, cozy mysteries, written mostly by women, that were housed in the Agatha Christie Room. They were lighter and more realistic to me.

Those were the books I wanted to write as well.

I smiled at the expression on Daniel's face. "Simon has been collecting books for years in anticipation of his shop."

"I think I've read about the debate regarding Mr. Canterville opening a book shop in this neighborhood. Wasn't there a formal complaint taken to the city council about proper zoning?"

It wasn't as though I didn't know about the problem, but it was different when he said it. It made me nervous, and when I was nervous, I had to find something to do with my hands. I walked quickly to the kitchen on the ground floor, filled the copper kettle, and turned the stove on under it.

"Yes. There has been a problem with one particular man, Ebenezer Hart. I've been to court with Simon during a few of the hearings. Mr. Hart apparently owns several properties here in Olde Town. He thinks there are too many commercial properties here now."

I put out china cups and saucers with a pretty, ivy pattern and then found honey, sugar, and several types of tea that I organized on the antique rosewood side table in the dining room. I could hear Admiral Leazer, Simon, and the others as they came inside, but it was Daniel's observant eyes on me that made my hands shake.

Crazy. Get hold of yourself. You're not his wife anymore.

"Why did Mr. Canterville hire you for this position, Lisa?" Daniel glanced around the kitchen. "You're kind of overqualified, aren't you, after all those years at the library? Were you laid off?"

I held my shoulders back and head high, despite the dark strand of hair that kept falling into my face. "I don't work for him. We're partners — my expertise with the books and other things related to running the shop, his house and money backing the venture."

"Really." His gaze flicked over me. "That's got to be like candy for you. It's what you always wanted to do. Congratulations."

"Thanks."

He took out a notebook. "Who's the man on the roof? How does he fit into the plan?"

"I have no idea." I knew I sounded stiff and unfriendly. "I couldn't see his face from the street."

"He's not on the roof any longer, Detective." Simon joined us at the rosewood table with Admiral Leazer and Mrs. Tappen right behind him. "Your coworkers have identified him, and it appears the Admiral was correct. He was most likely murdered."

"That's not all, Deputy Chief Fairhaven." The Admiral's voice was even louder than usual in the quiet dining room. "Canterville is leaving out the best part. The dead man is Ebenezer Hart, the one man who might have been able to stop him from making this place into a book shop."

Chapter Two

Tea and the Police

"Men's courses will foreshadow certain ends, to which, if persevered in, they must lead."

We sat together in the dining room — Simon, me, Mrs. Tappen, Admiral Leazer, and Daniel — while the police climbed over the house like ants with guns and badges.

Simon did remarkably well, considering he had a house full of people. He frowned as he concentrated on the cup of tea I had poured for him. "Are there almond cookies, Miss Wellman?"

"No, but they're on my shopping list," I replied.

"Shame about that."

"Is there cream, dear?" Mrs. Tappen asked.

"No, only milk. Sorry."

She wrinkled up her face as though I had suggested that she put mustard in the cup. This caused a thousand lines that weren't as easy to see to fan out from her eyes and mouth.

"I suppose that will have to do." She made a sour face as she tasted the tea. "Are you certain? There was cream in the fridge last time I was here. Excuse me." She slipped into the kitchen to rifle through the fridge.

Clearly she and Simon were much closer than I understood.

"If we could get back to the issue at hand," Daniel repeated for the third time.

Something crashed on the second floor. Simon blustered about imbeciles and lurched to his feet. I immediately got up and offered to see what had happened, gratefully leaving the tea table and running upstairs to the second floor.

The two police officers apologized for knocking down a stack of books. They'd already started piling them together again. Seeing hours of my work destroyed, I told them not to worry. They nodded and left me to it.

I was sitting on the floor separating the old copies of Hemingway and Melville when Daniel joined me.

"I thought you'd be asking questions downstairs." I hoped he'd take the hint.

"It's hard to talk around the Admiral." He sat beside me on the worn, red, Persian carpet. "Besides, I can't imagine either of the three of them killing Mr. Hart, at least not killing him and putting him on the roof. Can you? I don't think they'd have the strength for it."

I stopped separating books and glared at him. "Are you saying you can imagine me killing Ebenezer Hart?"

"No." He grinned as he picked up a copy of *Moby Dick*. "Of course not. But being an ex-librarian, I thought you might have some insight into what's going on."

"Into murder?" I snatched the book from him. "I saw Mr. Hart on the roof the same as everyone else. I didn't realize it was him until the Admiral said so. Despite his blustering, he might be the best person to question. How could he tell so easily that it was Mr. Hart? That's the question you should be asking."

"That's probably a good line of thought." He took out a small, new notebook from his jacket pocket. He had to peel away the plastic wrap from the blue cover. "This is my first homicide in a long time. I wasn't expecting to do it again."

"So why are you here?"

He grimaced and picked up another book. "Why are *you* here? Why aren't you working at the library?"

"Do you think that has something to do with Mr. Hart being dead? Honestly you have to stay on topic if you expect to find the answers you need."

"Because you know so much about solving homicides? I haven't done this in a few years, but I have more experience than you."

"I've read the best mysteries in the world." I took the second book from him. "And I'm a mystery writer now too. I've taken dozens of workshops. I'm working on my first book right now."

"Really? May I read some of it?"

"Of course not. It's bad luck to have anyone read your first manuscript before it's finished." I wondered what he was thinking. "Why are you here — really? You're being evasive."

Although, really, this plot wasn't a bad idea. I'd had trouble deciding how to kill my first victim. This had kind of dropped into my lap.

"I saw your name when I read the information about the death." Daniel got up from the floor. "I'd appreciate it if you could tell me what you know about the feud between Mr. Hart and Mr. Canterville."

"I'm sure you could get more information from the court documents that have been filed. There have also been several articles about it in the newspaper. It's been going on much longer than I've been here."

"Yes, but from a more personal perspective," he coaxed. "I'm sure you know everything that's going on."

I got to my feet and pushed the thick stacks of books against the wall to balance them. "I only know what I've heard, and that would be hearsay. Not much help to you. Detectives don't work that way, do they? I attended a seminar on how police detectives solve cases. Your father was there. He didn't teach the course, but his presence as the ex-police chief was impressive. Are you planning on taking his place?"

"I have a ways to go before Chief Masterson leaves. And I'm not sure that's what I want."

"A Fairhaven who doesn't want to be police chief, mayor, or District Attorney? Your family must think you're the black sheep now. When did you change? You wanted to be head of everything when we were together."

"I was more ambitious then." He shrugged. "Things change. Like you ending up here when all you ever wanted was to work at the library."

"You're right," I finally agreed. "Things do change."

Not that I wanted to go into how things had changed for me. He hadn't been part of my life in a long time, and he wouldn't be again once this was over.

"I really think you should ask someone else these questions." A police officer looked through books on one of the hundreds of shelves that had been recently installed. "The Admiral or Mrs. Tappen would know more than I do. I'm sorry I can't be of any real help to you."

The doorbell rang, and I moved to answer it. Simon's young English bulldog accompanied me, with his shallow attempts at barking. He saw the group at the table in the dining room and turned his attentions toward them as he tumbled down the last few steps, his stubby legs not quite able to reach them.

"Adam's Cable," the man at the door said when I opened it. He was wearing a yellow hardhat and tool belt covered with various cutters and wrenches.

"This might not be the best time," I told him. "Tomorrow might be better."

He pulled out an order book and a pencil that he licked before he started writing. "I'm going to have to call this in as a service refusal. I can't tell you when you'll get someone here again to install your cable, Mrs. Canterville. You'll have to call for another appointment, and I'm going to have to charge you for this call."

Daniel stepped up from behind her, showing his badge. "This is a police investigation. If you get in the way, you could be charged with obstruction. I think it would be in your own best interests to make another appointment with the Cantervilles."

The cable man nodded and put away his order book. "I'll check back, Officer. No need to make the situation any worse."

"Thank you." Daniel closed the front door.

"That was very nice of you." But suspicious. Why wouldn't he tell me why he was really there instead of a homicide detective? Why was he being so...helpful? What did he have in mind?

"You aren't really married to Simon Canterville, are you?"

"No." My face got hot. "Of course not. I told you that I'm his partner. I live here, but that's just part of it right now."

"And where does Mr. Canterville live?"

"In the basement. I live in the turret on the third floor."

He glanced up the stairs. "That's where Mr. Hart was, isn't it? Maybe we should take a look."

"Really? You really think it's necessary to look at my bedroom and office because Mr. Hart was found dead on the roof?"

"He had to get up there somehow, Lisa. Is there a window that opens up to the roof?"

"Yes, but—"

"Then I'm right behind you."

So that's what it is, I steamed, as I led the way upstairs. He was trying to throw me off because he wanted to know how the body got on the roof. I'd almost fallen for it. He was only doing his job. Wasn't that what I'd learned in my writing classes? I shouldn't take it personally, even though I could feel him looking at my backside as we went upstairs.

The third floor of the old house was only reachable by a spiral, wrought-iron staircase that went up from the second floor. It had been loose when I'd first arrived to take a look at things. Simon had someone come in the next day to tighten the bolts that held it in place. No one had been up there for years. There'd been a lot of clean up, but once it was done, I loved it.

My other cat, Maggie May, with her two-tone face and questioning eyes, watched us as we started up from the second floor. She moved aside as soon as she saw me go by. Jumping from stair to stair, she reached the third floor and looked down on us.

"How many cats live here?" Daniel asked from behind me.

"I brought two with me, but there was another, Puck, who'd been hanging around outside. He's a little feral, but I think he'll be okay. The bulldog pup belongs to Simon. I'm glad they all get along so well."

"Were you still living with your mother when you moved here?"

"No." I cringed, hoping he wouldn't ask any more about it. I wasn't ready yet. It was too soon to talk about my mother's death, especially with him.

I'd reached the third floor and waited for him to reach me. He shouldn't have made me feel all weepy just looking at him. The bond between us was broken. There weren't any of those feelings there anymore.

At least that was what I'd thought for the past twelve years, until I'd seen his face today.

We went through the door that reminded me of an old submarine entrance. It was metal, oval-shaped, and opened inside the room.

I was glad my room wasn't the disaster it usually was. I'd expected the cable man and hadn't known if he'd have to come up to put in a line for the internet. There was so much to do to get the house ready to open as a book shop. I hadn't really been prepared for it. Being a librarian meant I knew about books but not about running a book shop.

Still, Simon had offered me a chance to get back on my feet after the disaster my life had become. It was a place to live and work with books, which was why I'd become a librarian when my mother had told me I should be an accountant. It was also a secret place to hide from the world and watch from the windows as I contemplated my novel.

All the set-up would be done when the book shop opened, and then I'd have a lot more time to write. In the meantime, who wouldn't want to live in this wonderful, old house and have a chance to see and read so many books? It was a bibliophile's dream come true.

"I'm sorry about the clutter." Daniel stumbled over one of my suitcases that were still packed. "I've only been here a short time, and I've been busy with the book shop. Simon hopes to open by the end of November for Christmas."

He glanced around the room, taking in my desk with my old computer, the upholstered chair covered with clothes, and my unmade bed with Maggie May and Truffles on it.

The turret walls were set with three large windows

that looked down on the streets of Olde Town and the beautiful vista of the Elizabeth River. Dozens of quaint, older properties looked back at the Canterville house — which was part of the problem with Simon deciding to put a book shop in this cozy, residential neighborhood.

Ebenezer Hart had argued long and hard that Simon could put a book shop in the business area that was around the Olde Town neighborhood. But Simon had countered that he didn't own property in the business district. And besides, businesses, such as bed and breakfasts and a few doctors' offices, were already in the neighborhood.

Daniel peered out of the center window in the turret room. Just below him, a group of police officers had been joined by firefighters as they tried to lower the body from the roof. "You certainly had a clear view of what happened to Mr. Hart."

"I didn't see anything." I knew I sounded just like a suspect. I had motive — keeping my job with Simon. I wasn't sure when Mr. Hart had been killed, but it was probably during the night when my alibi was useless. That was all that was needed to make me look guilty.

Some parts of my brain were enjoying the whole thing. Where else would I get such a personal play-by-play of a murder investigation? I had a real-life police officer — albeit one that hadn't been in the field for a while — asking me questions about a man's death. If I was smart, I'd be recording the whole thing to play back as I wrote my novel.

He turned back from the window. "It's hard to imagine how someone got this body on the roof without waking you. It couldn't have been a quiet process."

"It may be because the house has steam heat," I conjectured. "It's been cold the last few nights, and the heat is noisy. I've had to learn to tune it out."

He came back toward me with his notebook in hand. "It would be easier than any means I can think of to drop the body from this window. Do you think it's possible that Simon Canterville killed Ebenezer Hart and dropped him from here? You just admitted that you've learned to desensitize yourself from the noise going on around you. Maybe you slept through this man's murder."

His words came with a dramatic flair, but I was still taken aback by his conjecture.

I carefully leveled my most steely gaze at him. It had been practiced many times at library patrons who'd insisted on talking though I'd asked them to be quiet.

"Simon Canterville wouldn't have the strength to heave Ebenezer Hart's body out the window without help. Look at the height of the window from the floor, and you can see it for yourself."

"Which brings me back to you. Where were you last night around eight p.m.? Was Mr. Canterville with you? That's the time the Admiral believes the murder took place."

Chapter Three

Just the Facts

"It is always the person not in the predicament who knows what ought to have been done in it, and would unquestionably have done it too."

I took a deep breath and faced my would-be opponent. It hardly seemed fair to have this discussion with him, since he obviously hadn't attended any mystery writer's workshops as I had for the past few years.

"Daniel."

"I'm sorry, Lisa. But you can see why I have to ask these questions."

"Daniel," I repeated, even throwing in a small

smile. "Don't you think it might be wise to wait for the preliminary autopsy? Obviously Mr. Hart didn't fall to his death, as he might have if he'd been thrown out the window. As we can both clearly see, he's still right here on the roof. That means he died from some other method and was carefully placed here. Without knowing what killed him, any theories based on what we already know would be useless."

"Wow. You do know a lot about homicide. Maybe you should apply to the police academy."

"No, thanks. My life is in these books. And my own work, of course."

"Which reminds me," he continued, verbally fencing with me. "I know you said it was bad luck to read your manuscript before it's finished. But what if you told me how your victim dies in your murder mystery? Does he or she get thrown off the roof?"

"I'm afraid that would keep me from finishing the book." I knew I sounded like a prig, but the truth was that I didn't know yet how my victim died. I didn't want him to know that. It made me sound like an amateur. "It's difficult to give parts of the story away without finding myself in limbo as I write. I'm a pantser, you know. I have to keep the story fresh."

"Pantser?"

"One who writes by the seat of her pants." I glared at him, hoping that settled the matter between us. "We should probably go back downstairs now. I'm sure Simon is wondering what's going on."

"After you." Daniel politely nodded toward the open door.

"Thank you for understanding."

I was so completely sure that he understood how

far ahead I was on this investigation that I was stunned when he told a police officer waiting outside the turret room to be sure to dust for fingerprints in my bedroom and have the crime scene team check for skin cells, blood, and clothing threads on the window sill.

"Go over the room thoroughly, please," he said to the officer. "The chances are the victim was tossed on the roof from here, even if he was killed somewhere else."

I went down to the second floor as quickly as I could. Was Daniel putting on an act to trap me into giving myself or Simon away as the killer? Anger, and a certain amount of admiration, surged through me as we reached the first floor. He was obviously more devious than I'd imagined.

Simon greeted me at the stairs. "I was wondering where you'd gotten off to, Miss Wellman. They are going through my bedroom and personal things. Perhaps we should consider consulting an attorney."

"You may be right. As in many mysteries where the protagonist is not a member of the police department, it's good to be protected." I glared at Daniel, who looked as sweet and innocent as a schoolboy. "Police detectives can be tricky."

"I'm sorry, Lisa," Daniel said. "This is my job."

"I understand that you misled me into thinking we were on the same side." I stepped around Simon, embarrassed, and walked away.

"You've upset her, lad," Simon said. "I believe you've done enough damage to my household for one day. Kindly leave the premises."

"It wasn't my intention to upset her, sir. I'm only trying to find the truth of what happened to Mr. Hart.

Perhaps if you told me where you were and what you were doing last night at about eight p.m., it might be helpful."

"Miss Wellman and I went out for a short walk. We can vouch for one another."

"I'm afraid that won't be enough, as you and Lisa might both be suspects. Did you see anyone while you were walking? You each had a good reason to want to see Mr. Hart dead. Did you kill him, and then she helped you throw him out the window to the roof?"

Simon laughed. "I believe I would be highly unlikely to tell you such a thing even if it were true."

"Then you see my dilemma. I know Lisa is grateful to you for giving her a place to stay. If you tell me what really happened, I can ask the DA to go easy on you for her sake. You'd be taking the brunt of the responsibility, you understand."

"Don't tell him anything, Mr. Canterville." I hastily rejoined them. "Call your lawyer. I don't think we can trust Daniel to tell us the truth."

"I'm sorry, Detective Fairhaven," Simon said. "But Miss Wellman is acting in both our best interests. Information that can be used against you and all that. Would you like another cup of tea? I can have her heat up the kettle again."

"No, thanks, sir." Daniel put away his notebook. "I'm going to speak with the officers outside. I'd appreciate it if you and Lisa remained in the house for now."

"We have some shopping to do. Perhaps after that we could pencil you into our schedule for a few moments."

"Please wait here," Daniel said. "And think about

what you want to say before I speak with you again for your sake and Lisa's."

An officer came inside and whispered something to Daniel before they both went outside. I saw an officer take up a position at the front door. It looked as though a trip to the grocery store would have to wait.

"Not to worry, Miss Wellman." Simon took my arm. "We'll shop later. For now, we can look over our new inventory list of books. There are new titles from the publisher. Makes one positively giddy with delight to contemplate it."

I was glad to go with him and put Mr. Hart — and Daniel — from my thoughts for a few minutes. The love of books was what had drawn Simon and me together. We talked for years at the library, sometimes every day. It wasn't anything personal, just about books we'd read.

Immediately after my mother had passed, less than a month ago, Simon had asked me to go into business with him. He'd told me about his plans for the book shop, and it had sounded wonderful, though I admit that I was looking for a place to get away.

He'd promised a place to live, food on the table, and all the books I could read while we set up and a forty percent share of the profits after we opened. I'd been skeptical. It would mean that I would have to quit the library. But in the end, I'd known that I needed the challenge and a place to stay, since I was going to have to sell my mother's house to pay for her medical expenses. I'd parked my Volkswagen Beetle in Simon's garage and hoped for the best.

It had been tricky getting my cats to believe this was their new home. I'd brought Puck in the first night.

Simon had been feeding him on the stoop in back. He wasn't happy about making that kind of change and commitment either. But more food than he'd ever seen at one time, and the enchantment of chasing Wordsworth finally convinced him that this was the right move for him too.

Truffles and Maggie May had been careful, thoroughly vetting every inch of the Victorian before settling in, but even they had found places to sleep by the end of the first day. Simon had hired a college student to help move my few possessions to the turret room and offered to help with selling the house. I knew this was my new home and was waiting for whatever life brought to me. I didn't think I'd ever been more afraid in my life.

The task of getting the old house ready to open as a book shop was monumental. Simon had to give up hundreds of antiques that wouldn't fit once we took the thousands of books he'd collected out of storage. He'd moved his bedroom to the basement, and we'd begun work on not only restoring parts of the house but putting up shelves and going through books.

Simon was an eclectic collector. He had dozens of copies of *John Carter of Mars* but no copies of *A Princess of Mars*. He had two full collections of everything Shakespeare had ever written. There were also duplicate copies of every Charles Dickens book and several copies of short stories written by Edgar Allen Poe.

"I don't recall reading a book by Agatha Christie." Simon took *Murder on the Orient Express* out of a box. "Must we include these titles written so recently?"

I laughed. "That book has been published for

decades. Surely it's earned its reputation as a classic."

"I'm not quite sure. Perhaps another few years would do it some good."

"We agreed that we'd have some newer authors too, Simon," I reminded him. "I'm only including newer titles that are popular and readers will be likely to ask for."

"Very well," he agreed grudgingly. "I'm certain I shall find some of these modern authors to my liking as well." He took out a copy of Stephen King's *Carrie*. "And what is this about?"

"It's considered horror," I answered. "But classic horror."

"Ah. Such as *Frankenstein* by Mary Shelley or *Dracula* by Brahm Stoker."

"Maybe a little more realistic." I took out several books from the box. "Maybe you should work your way up to King. He might be a little harsh for you."

Daniel found us separating and unpacking books in the front parlor. The whole room was filled with packed boxes that had yet to be opened. He cleared his throat.

"I'm sorry to disturb you," he said. "But it looks as though you were right about not moving too quickly into alibis from my pool of suspects."

"And why is that?" I asked.

"We now have cause of death from the medical examiner. It appears that Mr. Hart was shot."

"How terrible," I said, even though I was relieved. "I suppose that changes everything since Simon and I don't own any guns."

"That's a tricky supposition." He opened a bag he'd been carrying with gloved hands. "Mr. Hart was killed with an unusual weapon. Not something most people would own or have in working order these days. A French dueling pistol. From the smell of it, it's been fired recently."

Simon got to his feet and nodded at the weapon Daniel had. "I believe that is one of my pistols, Detective Fairhaven, a matched set given to me by my grandfather."

"I'm afraid that's completely true, sir. And it was found with your things in the basement. You'll have to come to the station with me."

Chapter Four

The Suspect

"Are these the shadows of the things that will be, or are they shadows of the things that may be only?"

It was ridiculous. Preposterous. There was no way that Simon Canterville could have been responsible for killing Mr. Hart.

Yet I had to watch him go as Daniel put him in the backseat of his car and drove away. His attorney was on the way to the house. I didn't want to leave until he arrived, not that Daniel had asked me if I'd wanted to go along.

"Such a pity." Mrs. Tappen shook her head. "Mr.

Canterville is a good man to have gone so wrong." She sighed as she started slowly toward her house.

"Good to see justice served." Admiral Leazer sounded satisfied as he watched them go.

"I hardly see this as being justice," I said. "You can't possibly believe Simon killed Mr. Hart. I know they didn't see eye-to-eye on the matter of the book shop. I've only known Simon a short time, but even I know he wouldn't hurt Ebenezer Hart. Why would he bother? He's never once doubted that he'd win the battle and open the shop."

The Admiral cleared his throat and straightened his shoulders. "I didn't expect you to understand, Miss Wellman. Murder tends to be a man's business. Best thing for you now is to look for other employment."

I refused to see the problem from his manly point of view. I glanced at my watch as the police stowed away their gear and prepared to leave the scene. The firefighters were already gone. The neighborhood seemed to be settling back into its normal mode, moving on without Simon and his newfangled ideas.

His lawyer, Bob Stanhope, slowly approached, pulling his shiny Cadillac into the drive. He leaned his well-coiffed, gray head out the window. He reminded me of a handsome ferret, if that was possible. He always seemed a little scatterbrained to be a lawyer.

"Miss Wellman?" he called out and waved to me. "What's going on? You said there was trouble. You didn't say it involved the police."

I climbed in the car with him. "Quick. We have to get to the police station. They've arrested Simon for murder."

But he didn't take off with a squeal of tires and the

smell of rubber as I hoped. Instead he calmly instructed me to tell him everything that had happened as he carefully checked his email on his phone.

That left me feeling more anxious and less like he was going to be able to take care of the situation. "Did you understand what I told you? The police think Simon murdered Mr. Hart, and they've taken him in for questioning."

"Of course I understand," he assured me. "I was sending a text to a friend of mine who works for the police department. Don't worry. We'll have him out in no time. We both know Simon isn't guilty of killing anyone. Who are they saying he killed, anyway?"

"Ebenezer Hart, the man against him opening the book shop? He was dead on the roof this morning." I thought I'd already explained this.

He let out a long low whistle. "That's not good. I should go to the police department to advise Simon."

"Yes, you should do exactly that. You're wasting your time here."

"It wasn't a waste of time, Miss Wellman. I'm better prepared now to help him."

I pulled the seatbelt across my lap. "That's more like it. Let's go."

Bob tried to talk me out of going. That wasn't happening. I mutinously sat in my seat, daring him to physically remove me. That was the only way I was getting out of his car.

The drive to the downtown police station was still too slow for me. He kept checking his texts, which made me nervous, and slowed down to stop at every yellow light. The trip took at least ten minutes longer than if I would've driven. I wouldn't want him to help me if there was an emergency.

Finally he parked his large, shiny car at the municipal parking lot, checked his hair in the mirror, and got out with his leather briefcase in hand. I got out too, prepared to go with him.

"There's no reason for you to go," he said. "I'll be back out in a jiffy."

"I'm going in. Whatever is going on isn't something I haven't seen. I was a librarian for over ten years.

He started to speak and then shook his head. "Whatever you like. Just stay out of the way and keep your mouth shut. Anything you say could be harmful to Simon's case."

I started to answer back that I would never do anything to hurt Simon but did as he requested. The lawyer and I had only spoken a few times in the two weeks I'd been involved with opening the book shop. I wasn't particularly fond of the man, but Simon spoke of him as being excellent at his job. That was all that mattered right now. I didn't want Simon to have to spend the night in jail.

My knees shook as we went inside the police station. I knew I hadn't done anything wrong, and I'd been in this station on a tour with other mystery writers. But this was different, knowing that Simon was in trouble and I couldn't help him.

Yes, we'd only been something more than acquaintances for a short time, but he already meant a lot to me. It felt like we were two drifters off to see the world, like in the old "Moon River" song from *Breakfast at Tiffany's*. There may have been a huge age gap between us, but we were kindred spirits. We both loved books, old movies, Audrey Hepburn, French toast, antiques, and so much more. I couldn't allow this terrible thing to happen to him.

"What do we do now?" I whispered as we approached the desk with a frowning police sergeant behind it.

"Leave it to me. Just sit down and be quiet. Everything will be fine."

I did as he said, watching people walk in and out of the lobby. I was hoping to see Simon or even Daniel, but I didn't see anyone I knew. An old man sat beside me and asked me if I wanted to buy a watch from him. I didn't have the five dollars he wanted, but he took the two dollars I had for it.

Bob was only gone a few minutes when he came back to the lobby. He put one finger to his lips as I started asking questions. We walked outside before he started talking.

"I'm afraid this is going to be much harder than I thought." His frown wrinkled his older, but admittedly handsome face. "The police have the murder weapon, which belongs to Simon and was found in his possessions. He has no alibi for the time when they think Mr. Hart was killed. And he had every reason in the world to see him dead. It's difficult when the police hold all the cards."

"I'm his alibi," I protested. "He and I were together around the time the police said Mr. Hart was killed."

"I'm afraid that you have a vested interest in this, Miss Wellman. The police aren't going to take your word for his whereabouts. I'm sorry."

"Are they letting him go? Does he need money to make bail? Once we get him out, we can start looking for real answers. I'm telling you—he didn't kill anyone."

"I know." He shook his head and glanced at his cell phone. "I have to be in court in less than an hour. I can't do much right now. I'll call his son and see if there's anything he can do. I'm afraid the bail might be quite high."

"Why?" I knew about this part of a murder investigation too. "He's been part of the community for his whole life, and I don't think he's even had a speeding ticket, has he? He drives that Bentley at twenty miles under the speed limit. Surely he's not a flight risk."

"It's difficult to explain to someone who doesn't have legal experience. The best thing you can do right now is go back to the house and wait for me to call you."

"But—"

"Really, Miss Wellman. Either I or Simon's son will get in touch with you."

He offered me a ride to the bus stop so I could get home while he was in court. I turned him down and waited in the police station just in case something else came up.

It took me a moment or two to process what he'd said.

Simon had a son.

This was the first I'd heard of it. It seemed there were other things we hadn't talked about. Books and Audrey Hepburn were wonderful, but there were real things that mattered.

Why wouldn't he have told me?

I wasn't sure what else I could do until I saw

Daniel come into the station. I jumped up right away and pulled at his jacket sleeve to get his attention. "Can you help me? I'd like to see Simon."

He was startled to see me and took a quick glance around him as though to check who else had noticed. "Come with me."

I followed him through a long hall and a maze of small offices. It looked nothing like police stations I'd seen on TV. They hadn't taken us this far on the tour. We finally reached a small office that he opened and let me enter before him. I took a chair and waited for him to sit down. My patience was beginning to wear thin, and I was scared.

"Why are you here?" he asked as he carefully maneuvered himself behind the desk and pushed aside a mound of papers. The room was tiny, barely enough space for the desk and two chairs. He had to move the trash can out of the way to sit down.

And he's the Deputy Chief?

"I told you. I want to see Simon, and I want to know what I can do for him."

"His lawyer has already been here, Lisa. He'll do what needs to be done."

"There has to be something else. If his lawyer moves any slower, Simon will be in here forever. What can I do? Can I testify for him? Of course, that would mean waiting until the trial. His lawyer didn't seem to think it was likely that he'd get out on bail. Has he officially been charged?"

"There isn't anything you can do right now," Daniel said. "He hasn't been officially charged with Mr. Hart's murder, but it seems likely that he will be. The evidence is damaging. We're waiting for forensics on the dueling pistol."

"That may be true," I replied. "But he's not guilty."

"You said yourself you couldn't swear that Mr. Hart's body didn't go out your window. How can you be so sure Mr. Canterville didn't kill him?"

"Because I know him. He wasn't worried about Ebenezer Hart, Daniel. He's not like that. He believes that everything will be fine. You saw the house. Did that look like someone who thought there might not be a book shop lived there?"

He straightened some papers on his desk. "Lisa, sometimes good people do bad things. It happens very quickly. Many people insist it's a moment of insanity. It can happen to anyone."

I was wasting my time. I could see that he couldn't be convinced of Simon's innocence. But I couldn't simply go back to the house and wait to see what would happen. It wasn't in my nature.

"Thank you for your help. I'm sure everything will be all right."

He got to his feet. "I know that look."

"What look?"

"That one where your mouth turns down and your cheeks puff out. It always preceded an argument when we were married."

"That was a long time ago," I informed him as regally as possible.

"You aren't planning to do something we'll both regret, are you?"

"I'm not sure what you mean by that."

"Like breaking him out of jail or threatening the judge who has his bail hearing." He pointed a finger at me. "You don't just give up."

"I guess I do this time. Simon's lawyer is incompetent, but I guess he'll have to do."

Daniel still eyed me suspiciously, but what else could he say? I hadn't done anything wrong. That hadn't stopped him from locking up Simon, but they didn't need two suspects.

"All right. Do you need a ride back to the house?"

"No, I can find my own way back. Thanks anyway."

"Oh, for heaven's sake. It's just a ride back to the house. I've got a few minutes before they need anything else from me. Let me take you home."

I finally agreed, just to keep him from badgering me. He thought he knew me—I definitely knew him. He'd think nothing of following me back to the house in a squad car with the lights and sirens on. Daniel loved grand gestures. He'd proposed to me dressed as Santa in a crowded department store.

We left the station in his shiny, brown Ford. It was such a mess inside that it took him a few minutes to get everything off the front seat so I could get in. He hadn't changed, at least in that respect.

"I know this isn't you." He glanced at me when we stopped at a light. "What are you hoping to gain?"

"I'm hoping to gain the dream of a lifetime. Cataloguing Simon's collection and helping him set up his shop is a wonderful opportunity for me. I know you don't understand, since the mere mention of a book title puts you to sleep. But this is exciting, and it offers me a challenge I've always wanted."

He shook his head. "Is something wrong with you? Are you dying from some fatal brain-eating disease? All you ever wanted when we were married is to have a house, two kids, and a husband who came home for dinner every night. What happened to that Lisa Wellman?"

"Things change." I carefully looked him over. "What happened to the man who never wanted to have a desk job? 'I never want to leave the street.' I thought that mantra was engraved on your heart—or your revolver. Oh wait. That *is* your heart."

It wasn't a long drive from police headquarters to Olde Town. Thank goodness. If we'd been alone in a car too much longer, something really bad might have happened.

"I'm still wondering why you showed up at the crime scene." I said as he parked the car at the curb. "You have detectives for that, don't you?"

Daniel took a deep breath. "I go where Chief Masterson tells me to go."

"I see." He was lying. I didn't know why but I could tell by the tone of his voice and the expression on his face. I got out of the car and glanced back at him. "Will you let me know when Simon is officially charged?"

"Sure."

I took out my cell phone, but he hadn't moved. "Do you need something to write down my number? Or can we put the phones together, and it will show up on your phone?"

"Don't worry about it."

"What does that mean?" It suddenly occurred to me. "You know my number, don't you?"

"I know a lot of people's numbers. Don't make a big deal out of it."

"That number has changed a dozen times since we

split up. I don't even have the same cell phone company. Have you been spying on me?"

"I don't spy on people." He started the car again. "I'll see you later. Do yourself a favor—move back to your own place and get another job. I don't see Simon Canterville getting out of this without a long stay in prison. You backed a losing horse this time."

"I guess that's my weakness," I shot back at him. "I have a thing for losers."

He nodded and pulled away. I turned back to face the lovely, old house that was covered in crime scene tape. People stood on the sidewalk gawking at it and taking pictures with their cell phones. It was completely depressing.

Mrs. Tappen was out there, of course. She was talking to the Admiral, no doubt reminiscing about all the things Simon did that they thought were stupid because they made no sense to them. I managed to skirt by them without being seen and make it into the house. I stood with my back against the door, Daniel's words ringing in my ears.

Had I given up everything only to lose Simon Canterville?

Chapter Five

The Son and Heir

"There are many things from which I derived good by which I have not profited."

It took only a minute for Wordsworth to sound his husky, puppy *woof*, which alerted the cats that someone was home. I patted his head and put out some food for him. By that time, Truffles and Maggie May were wondering why their bowls were empty. I fed them too and convinced Puck to eat something next to the kitchen door. He hissed at me when I tried to scratch his ears.

"You'll come around," I told him as I made a cup of

tea for myself. It reminded me that we were supposed to shop for food, and that made me want to cry.

Why was this happening? I had to pull myself together. Simon was helping to make my dream come true. I had to figure out what was needed to help him.

My mystery writing seminars had prepared me for this. All I had to do was think who else would want to kill Ebenezer Hart. Obviously the man had enemies. He was loudmouthed and obnoxious. He'd probably made other people angry over his tactics. I knew he was an attorney. No one liked them, did they?

I grabbed a pad of paper and started writing. I had to find out who possibly disliked and wanted to kill Mr. Hart. Daniel had at least shared the information about the gun that had killed him. If it really was one of Simon's dueling pistols, that meant that he was purposely being set up to take the fall.

That was a whole other plotline.

"Someone wanted the police to think that Simon was responsible for killing Mr. Hart," I said to Wordsworth. "They also wanted the police to think Simon was stupid enough to leave the body on his own roof. They don't know him at all, do they?"

Wordsworth covered the brown spot on his face with his little paws and groaned.

"I feel exactly the same way." I looked at what I'd written and puzzled over it. "It had to be someone who could get in and out of the house without being noticed—someone with a key, perhaps, and a reason to get rid of Simon, without killing him instead."

The front door opened immediately as I finished speaking. A strange man I didn't recognize in his mid-forties or early fifties, thick, graying, black hair, and long legs in jeans strolled in. He smiled as he scanned the front foyer and parlor area.

"Yes? Can I help you?" I crossed my arms over my chest. Wordsworth growled, and Truffles hissed. "The book shop isn't open yet. Are you with the police?"

He looked surprised to see me there. "Hello. Why are you here?"

"I'm Miss Wellman. I work here. Who are you?"

"I'm Ashcroft Canterville. This is my father's house. You work for him?"

The long-lost son I'd only heard about that morning.

"Yes." I walked toward him and offered him my hand. "I'm afraid your father isn't here right now. He ran into some bad luck this morning."

Ashcroft absently shook my hand and kept walking past me, his gaze moving around the rooms as though he was looking for something. "Yes. I heard. It's all over the news. A shocking turn of events."

"I'm so sorry you had to hear about it that way. I would've called to let you know, but Simon hadn't mentioned you. I only heard about you from his lawyer. I guess he called you."

"Where is all the furniture?" He closely examined the blank spot on the floor between the new bookshelves. So much for him being devastated by what had happened to his father.

"Simon put that away in preparation of visitors to the shop. Some of it is valuable."

"And where is it?"

"That's not for me to say." I lifted my chin to be more equal to his gaze that was several inches above mine. He had his father's height but obviously not his heart. "Would you like a cup of tea?"

"No, Miss Wellman." He finally stopped scrutinizing the walls and floor. "What I'd like is for you to leave. I'm sorry. I know this is hard on you, and it's happened very quickly. But I doubt my father will be going into business selling books anytime soon. You can go back to wherever he found you. You won't be digging any of my inheritance out of him anytime soon."

My first impulse was to smack him. The little snot was only here to take what Simon owned. He was examining the rosewood table in the dining room now, opening the drawers where the silver was kept.

Really?

But I managed to hold back my hand and my temper. I wasn't going to let him force me into making a mistake I'd regret later. Instead I stared at him until he glanced back at me.

"You're still here?"

"I'm a partial owner in this enterprise," I told him. "Your father and I have a contract that I would be happy to have my lawyer enforce." Simon and I did have a contract. Well, more a strong verbal agreement, but Ashcroft didn't have to know that.

His blue eyes that were so like Simon's, and yet so different, gazed back at me in anger and frustration. "I'm sure we can work this out. After all, you won't want to be here with my father gone. How much would it take to buy out your portion of the book shop contract?"

"I wouldn't take a thing for it until I know for sure what's going to happen to your father. If you cared anything about him, you'd be at the police station right now looking after his welfare, not worrying about where his valuables are kept."

Ashcroft smiled in a sleazy manner. "The old man can take care of himself. Trust me. I know. He and I have never been close, but I know he'd want me to take possession of his house and personal effects for him while he's otherwise occupied, even if it's only for safekeeping until he gets out of prison."

I thought about my suspect list. One fine instructor—and a wonderful mystery writer—had told me that all mystery writers needed a good suspect list. Clearly Ashcroft Canterville had to be on that list.

1. He obviously disliked his father and possibly wouldn't hesitate to frame him for murder.

2. He had motive and maybe opportunity, since he'd let himself into the house. No doubt he had a key. Where was he when Mr. Hart was killed, anyway?

3. He had as many reasons to see his father go to prison as the police thought Simon had for killing Mr. Hart.

"I'm sorry you had to come all this way to find yourself with a lost cause, Ashcroft. But if you don't leave now, I'll be forced to call the police. Considering that they were recently here, I don't think it will take long to return."

"Good. I can have them throw you off my property. I've tried being nice about this. I don't have to be. Call the police." He taunted me with an expression that dared me to do as he said.

Was he correct? Just how strong was the agreement between me and Simon? I was so thrilled to venture into this enterprise that I didn't question as much as I should have. I'd sold everything to be part of the book shop. Panic set in as I wondered what I was going to do now.

"Ashcroft!" Simon's voice rang out from the doorway. "What are you doing here?"

I ran to his side, feeling like a distressed maiden character. "I'm so glad you're back. How did it happen?"

"The police released me, Miss Wellman. A spot of tea would be most welcome. All they offered me were those horrid, fizzy drinks the young people enjoy so much these days. Will you join us, son?"

"Oh, father." Ashcroft came to his side, wiping a fake tear from his eye. "I was so worried when I heard that you'd been arrested. I'm so happy you're home."

My lips felt tight as I longed to tell Simon exactly how worried his son had been about him. I realized that there would be time later after Ashcroft had crawled back under his rock. I glanced up as I started toward the kitchen for tea and noticed Daniel standing in the doorway behind Simon.

As the father and son spoke in muted tones, I stepped around them to talk to Daniel. "I'm surprised to see you here."

"He needed a ride home. There was no reason to assign it to an officer when I already knew where he was going."

"How did he get out? What happened?"

"Are you inviting me in for tea too?"

"All right. But only if there's a detailed explanation of what happened."

"You know, I don't remember you being so hard, Lisa."

"Not like you ever really knew me," I retorted.

"Don't just stand there with the door open. I'll get the tea. We have coffee too, if you'd rather."

"Yes." He grinned. "I'll take the coffee."

Glad that we'd managed to get the front door closed before the Admiral or Mrs. Tappen also had to join us, I got hot water boiling and coffee brewing quickly. The milk that had been on the table from earlier was gone. Maggie May bumped against my leg with what always appeared to be a smile on her half-gray, half-white face.

I knew who'd managed to get to the milk first.

"You've had enough," I told her as I cleaned out the creamer and poured more milk in it.

Ashcroft, Daniel, and Simon were all sitting at the table as I brought in the cups on a tray. Simon was unusually quiet. I hoped the time he'd spent at the city jail hadn't been too much for him.

"Coffee." I put the cup in front of Daniel.

Simon and Ashcroft were already taking their cups of tea.

I took a cup too and sat beside Simon. "So what happened? Not that I'm not happy that you're here, but why did they release you?"

"Miss Wellman." Ashcroft made it sound like a rebuke. "You don't sound particularly enthusiastic about my father's release."

"I'm sure I'm more enthusiastic than you are," I snapped back.

Simon nodded. "I'm glad you're both worried about me. But no reason for it. Justice prevailed. The police saw the error of their ways."

"In other words," Daniel explained. "The French dueling pistol that shot Mr. Hart might not have been the same pistol we took from Mr. Canterville's bedroom."

"What?" Ashcroft spilled his tea in his haste to put his cup back on his saucer. "How many antique, French dueling pistols are there in Portsmouth?"

"He didn't mention that it was antique!" I pounced on his words.

"What else would it be?" His glance appealed to his father.

"Believe me, I felt the same way," Daniel said. "But apparently the forensics are more complicated on antique weapons. The results were inconclusive."

"What are the odds?" Ashcroft demanded.

"Is there something you want to tell us about Mr. Hart's murder?" I asked him.

"No." His expression was defensive. "I was only surprised, that's all. I'm glad for the outcome, of course."

He was still on my suspect list.

"Well, thanks for the coffee." Daniel got to his feet, only a few sips from his cup. "If you could walk me out, Lisa."

"Yes. I could do that." What did he want now?

I followed him to the door, leaving Ashcroft at the rosewood table with Simon.

"Don't make any long-term plans with Mr. Canterville. He's out now on a technicality, but I have a feeling it won't be for long."

Chapter Six

The Ghost

"There is more of gravy than of grave about you, whatever you are!"

I didn't reply, just nodded and watched him leave. I didn't believe a word of it. Simon was a kind and gentle man. If he had a temper, I'd never seen it as we worked together. He was the champion of rescue animals and supported a homeless shelter. He could converse about almost every book in every category. I'd never met his match.

Daniel had no idea what Simon was really like. But his warning left me believing that the police weren't finished investigating him. Maybe the gun didn't match up, but that didn't mean there weren't other circumstances that still made him a person of interest.

I knew what that meant too—the police would be watching him and continuing to look for ways that he could've been responsible for Mr. Hart's death. It would be annoying and put off our clientele when we opened the book shop if it wasn't resolved.

In the meantime, I was going to have to decide about Ashcroft. He could have been the killer. I was going to have to look into his whereabouts last night. It teased my mind what he'd gain by framing his father for murder, but there could be a motive there somewhere. Maybe it was just that he wanted the house before it was made into a book shop. Maybe he wanted everything, which would happen if Simon went to jail.

Ashcroft left with a scowl on his face a short time later. It didn't appear that he and Simon had been arguing, but I wasn't sure.

"I thought he'd never leave," Simon said with a sigh as the door closed behind his son.

"It was surprising when he came in and told me who he was. Bob told me you had a son as we were going to the police department."

"And I am sorry I didn't mention him before, Miss Wellman. I haven't seen him in at least a year. I didn't realize he'd come 'round when I was arrested for murder. Of course, I had no plans to be arrested for murder."

"That's all right. We all have people that we'd like to forget."

He raised one white brow. "As you have tried to

put the Deputy Chief from your thoughts."

"Well…" I averted my eyes before I gave too much away. "I'm not even sure why he turned up today. He hasn't been a homicide detective in a few years."

"Can't you imagine why he might want to see you again?" He grinned and rocked back on his heels. "I certainly can."

"Well, now you know about Daniel, and I know about Ashcroft. I guess that makes us ready to move on."

"I would say so," he agreed. "I believe we were going through these boxes of new books when we were so rudely interrupted."

That was something I could handle.

For the rest of the day, we ignored further police and crime scene teams continuing to go over the house as we sorted through many of my favorite titles and authors. We paused briefly for some scrambled eggs and toast for dinner, talking the whole time about what we needed for the shop and our plans for the future.

"We should order one of those nice, silver cash registers," he said. "I saw one recently in a magazine. Shall I purchase one? I could imagine it being on a table right there by the window."

"Actually, I was thinking about this new device that runs off a tablet — like a small computer. It scans books and credit cards and would help us keep track of how much money we've made."

"Credit cards?" he frowned. "Do we plan to accept anything but cash?"

I laughed at the suggestion that we could only do business with cash. "Most people shop with credit cards now. We don't want to lose those sales."

"Quite, my dear. I shall bow to your expertise in this matter. Although I would truly love to have one of those towering, silver cash registers. We could use it for those people who are paying with cash. I have never had a credit card in my life."

"That's fine. I'm sure it will be impressive. We have other antiques, why not an antique cash register?"

Simon yawned and glanced at the grandfather clock against the wall. It was barely eight p.m. "I believe the day has gotten the better of me, Miss Wellman. I should like to turn in now and start fresh tomorrow."

"That's fine. I'm a little tired myself."

"Goodnight. Sleep well." He took one of the new books, a Louise Penny mystery, with him. "I believe I should begin to read books from this day and age so I might converse intelligently with our customers."

I hugged him, always aware of his thin body and frail form. "I read that book last month. You and I can talk about it when you finish."

"Very good." He shook his finger at me. "No spoilers."

After Simon disappeared behind the door into the basement, I made sure all the doors were locked securely. I didn't feel quite as secure as I had the night before, when there hadn't been a dead man on the roof in the morning and I hadn't known that Ashcroft was a gold digger with a key.

But there was only so much I could do. Wordsworth would bark if he heard anything unusual. The problem was that his puppy bark was more like a cough and would hardly be noticeable. I decided to talk with Simon the next day about an alarm system. It was way past time that he should have had one anyway. With the shop opening and thousands of dollars in books besides his valuable antiques, we definitely needed one.

I had to admit that this was my favorite time of day. I went quickly upstairs to the turret room after the downstairs lights were shut off. Truffles and Maggie May followed me. Puck still preferred to sleep by the kitchen door. I put on my pajamas and slid into the chair in front of my laptop. It was time to pick up my story where I'd left off.

The events of the day played havoc with the characters in my mind. April Fitzhugh was my main character. She'd awakened in a large, dark house on the coast of Virginia during a hurricane. She was totally alone and terrified because all she could recall was her name.

As I scrolled though the first fifty pages of my manuscript, I realized there was too much narrative and not enough dialogue. It would be difficult to have dialogue in a book with only one character. Maybe she could talk to herself.

Or she might find a stray cat huddled inside the creepy, old mansion, hiding from the storm.

April's dialogue began to take shape as she found the shivering cat and wrapped him in a towel to dry him. This could work. It could still only be April in the old house with the storm, but she could let the reader know what she was thinking without having someone else to talk to. I needed a name for the cat.

"Oh, Buttercup," April said. "At least I have you."

No. Not Buttercup. I deleted that name.

"Oh, Sage," April said. "At least I have you."

There was a dull scraping noise in the hall outside my room. For a moment I thought it was in the story, but then I realized that it was real. I ignored it, thinking it was probably just the cats and the books. I'd straighten it out tomorrow.

"Oh, Evelyn," April said. "At least I have you."

It occurred to me—if April didn't know anything but her own name, how would she know the cat's name?

Another tumble of books drew my attention away from my story. The cats were getting carried away. It would take all day to clean up their mess. I got to my feet, but Maggie May and Truffles were asleep on the bed. Wordsworth never came up to the third floor. His short legs wouldn't allow him to get up on the spiral staircase.

Rats? I hadn't noticed any since I'd been there, but it was possible. I turned on the lights in my room and flicked on the hall light before I ventured out with a heavy fireplace poker.

"What the—" The words came out barely above a whisper.

The books had sounded like they were falling, but two huge stacks, taller than me, were in the hall. I'd just looked at them as I'd gone by on my way to the bedroom. I was sure they weren't there.

It had to be Ashcroft. He was playing some kind of stupid prank that he hoped would drive me out of Simon's life.

"You've got to be kidding," I said with more force, now that I realized what was happening. "You really think this is going to scare me?"

It had frightened me, at least to begin with. Now

that I understood, I wasn't scared at all.

"I'm calling the police." I used the fireplace poker to smack the palm of my hand. "And you better hope I don't find you before they get here."

There was no response. He was probably hiding in one of the rooms. I didn't give him the satisfaction of searching randomly for him so he could jump out at me. Instead I stalked back into the bedroom, angry because he was wasting my writing time.

I picked up my cell phone and gave him one last chance.

"Okay. This is it. This is me calling the police." I walked to the doorway before I dialed 911 and glanced back into the hall.

And dropped my cell phone on the thick, new carpet Simon had installed in my room.

The books that had been in the tall piles were gone. Just like that. Vanished. Hundreds of books missing. I didn't see them anywhere in the hall.

It wasn't possible. Ashcroft couldn't have unstacked and moved those books somewhere else so quickly. I bent to the floor and grabbed my phone before I fled back into my room and locked the door behind me.

"What's going on?" I asked the cats, much like my character in the book. "Even if Ashcroft wanted to scare me, he couldn't have done that. It's just not possible."

That was when something hard slammed against the outside of the bedroom door. I ran to the other side of the room and hunkered down near the window. I was thinking I could jump out on the roof if I had to. I held my cell phone in my shaking hand before me like a gun until I realized what I was doing. As I heard another thud against the door, I grabbed the fireplace poker again and brandished it before me like a sword.

"I called the police," I shouted. "They're going to be here in a few minutes. You'd better leave now if you know what's good for you."

The cats were calmly licking their paws and cleaning themselves with all the devotion cats usually put into their grooming. They were ignoring everything that was happening. As two more loud thumps hammered against the door, I decided it was time to stop warning Ashcroft. He'd find out now that I wasn't joking about calling the police.

I tapped 911 into the keypad as several more thumps occurred.

"911 operator. What is your emergency?"

"This is Lisa Wellman at 459 Middle Street in Olde Towne. Someone has broken into my home and is threatening me."

"This is the 911 operator. Can you speak?"

"Yes. I'm telling you someone is in my house."

"Look. It's illegal to prank call 911. You could be arrested or fined for doing this."

"Arrest me," I yelled desperately. Why couldn't she hear me? "Just send someone over here."

The operator took a deep breath and hung up.

I tried to call again. This time there was no response at all.

But that was the least of my worries. The locked bedroom door slowly unlocked and then began to open. I thought about Ashcroft's front-door key. Of course he could get in here, I thought hysterically. He could come right in and kill me then throw me off the roof as he probably had Mr. Hart. I was a goner. Even my cats were ignoring me.

There was only one thing to do. I had to climb out on the roof before he could kill me first. The worst that would happen is that I might slip and fall to the ground. How high was I, anyway? I struggled to recall the Death From On High workshop I'd taken in Wilmington at the Cape Fear Crime Festival that had described what happened to people who fell to their deaths.

Pushing my frozen limbs into motion, I dropped the fireplace poker and shoved my cell phone into the pocket of my pajamas. I was going to have to try not to land on my right side and break my phone. I'd still need it to call for help—hopefully more successfully than I'd done here.

I pushed open the window. It stuck on the wooden sill, but I pushed harder as the door continued to squeak open behind me. I glanced down at the front yard, illuminated by the new lighting put in so the book shop could stay open in the evening. It was a long way down. Definitely broken bones and a concussion. If I could avoid the concrete sidewalk and aim for the bushes, I might be able to deflect some of the damage.

With one leg in and one leg out, I waited to be sure that it was Ashcroft. I didn't want to jump if I didn't have to. My heart pounded so fast that I was afraid I might have a heart attack before he could push me out the window.

The door continued slowly opening—so slowly that I began to wonder if Wordsworth had actually found a way up the spiral staircase and was nosing it open. That didn't explain the lock opening in the middle of the door, but my mind was trying to think of anything else that made sense.

Finally it pushed open the remaining few inches. There seemed to be a glowing image there, revealed much like moonlight would light a statue in a garden. I could tell it was the shape of a man in clothing from the 1800s. His hair stood up on his head, and a scarf was wrapped around his jaw. Heavy, glowing chains were wrapped around his body.

He started moving into the room dragging the chains behind him, moaning piteously as he came. "Oh, woe is me. Oh, woe, that I must walk the streets I did not walk when I was alive. Oh, woe. Poor damned soul for all eternity."

Wait. This was something I'd seen before. It wasn't Ashcroft or Wordsworth. This was a scene from a movie.

"I've seen this." I snapped my fingers. "*A Christmas Carol*. You're Jacob Marley from *A Christmas Carol*."

He continued moaning, ignoring me, as he came further into the room. The chain was loud as it scraped the floor. It also made a clanking sound as it hit against itself.

"What is this? Are you advertising for the play? How did you get in here?" It was remarkable the things a mind could think of in a few seconds when properly motivated by fear.

He stopped walking and slowly looked up at me. "I am the ghost of Jacob Marley. I wear the chains I forged in life. You have only the slightest chance of ever becoming a serious writer, and I am here to help you."

Chapter Seven

What's New?

"With affection beaming out of one eye and calculation out of the other."

I brought one leg back from the roof.

"Wait. What?" I picked up the fireplace poker again. "Barry, is that you? Is this some kind of weird practical joke?"

Barry was in the weekly writer's group I attended. This was just like him since his writing had a flare for the melodramatic.

But how did he get into the house? We definitely needed a security system. Everyone was going in and out like a bus depot.

He stopped moving so that the chains stopped rattling. "Do you not hear well then, girl? I have told you my name. I do not know a man named Barry, if there is indeed such a person."

"I'm afraid there is more of gravy than of grave about you, sir," I quoted from *A Christmas Carol*. "How'd you get in here? I'll bet you sneaked in with the police."

"How now?" The man before me threw off his chains and pulled the rag from around his head.

I looked away quickly, knowing it was supposed to hold his jaw up.

He looked at the rag before he threw it to the floor, along with the chains that had wrapped around him. "Do you not believe in ghosts then?"

"No, I don't believe in ghosts, Barry, and you're starting to annoy me. If you get out now, I'll give you a five-minute head start before I call the police."

"What can I say that will convince you that I am indeed a ghost and not the inestimable Barry? Is this your young man? I tell you now that writing your novel will be much harder if you allow love to get in the way."

I brought the other leg inside too. "That's it. I'm calling the police. You've completely lost it. And don't bother telling me that you're doing this for that stupid Christmas play you're in."

"A play?" He looked eager. "I adore plays. Which of the bard's plays are being staged at this time? My favorite is *A Twelfth Night*. I suppose you are partial to *Romeo and Juliet*, being of a romantic nature."

"Not Shakespeare, and you know it, Barry." I

redialed 911. "It's *Scrooged* from Charles Dickens. Why am I even bothering to tell you? You know what play you've been bragging about for the past month."

"*Scrooged*?" His features took on a puzzled stare. "Ah! An adaptation of *A Christmas Carol*, no doubt. How wonderful that some ignoramus writer with no more sense than a rock decided he could rewrite the masterpiece I left behind."

The 911 operator answered again. "What is your emergency?"

"My emergency?" he yelled at me. "My emergency is seeing my work cut to pieces as lesser men try to make sense of it. Abominable!"

"What is the emergency?" the operator demanded again.

"There's a man in my bedroom who doesn't belong here, and he's crazy. Send the police."

"Listen—if this is the same prank caller from earlier—when I have them trace your call, you're going to jail." And she hung up.

"Stupid cell phone." I hit it with my hand. "I pay a fortune for service, and where is it when I need it?"

My glowing visitor heaved a heavy sigh. "Like Scrooge himself, I see you must be convinced that I am a visitor from the hereafter. So be it."

As I watched, he rose through the air to the ceiling above me. The chains were gone, but he shrieked loudly and waved his arms around.

It was so terrifying that my cats all ran downstairs without waiting to see if I was going too. But I was right behind them. I stubbed my toe on the iron staircase, but that didn't stop me. I made it to the second floor. My feet didn't touch the stairs as I flew down to the first floor.

I rested against the front door and waited to see what would happen. If it really was Barry, I was going to hit him hard with something when he came down. I wasn't sure how it could be him, but it made more sense than a ghost dressed like Jacob Marley.

"You're fortunate you didn't kill yourself racing down the stairs that way," he said from right above me. "People these days are certainly different than they were in my time. When the spirit of my dead mentor came to me, I prostrated myself on the floor. Thus I did the same in my novel with Scrooge when he was visited by Marley. But not you. Instead you run willy-nilly, trying to elude me when common sense declares that one cannot run from a ghost."

I had never screamed at a mouse, snake, spider, or any other creature in my life. But while he spoke to me, I screamed for all I was worth. The cats hissed, and Wordsworth finally began to bark, such as it was.

Simon's footsteps came up the basement stairs. He opened the door into the kitchen. "All right. I know you're here. Come out now if you know what's good for you."

Not wasting a moment, I ran into the kitchen. "Thank goodness you're awake."

He glanced down at me with a raised brow as he slowly put down his antique sword. "My dear Miss Wellman. Are you engaged in some sort of fit? Has someone broken into the house?"

"There's a ghost," I told him, pointing at the ghost that had followed me. "I think he believes he's Charles Dickens."

Simon's eyes calmly scanned the ceiling. "Is he here

with us now?"

"Yes. He's floating right there in front of us with a kind of evil smirk on his face."

"I am neither smirking nor evil," the ghost declared. "And I do not believe myself to be the spirit of the greatest writer of the nineteenth century—I am he."

"He's talking right now," I told Simon. "Can't you see him or hear him?"

"You have obviously been overwrought by the events of the day." Simon patted my shoulder. "I suggest a drop of whiskey for each of us and a return to our beds. Tomorrow things will look much brighter."

He went to the side cabinet he used to store liquor and took out two small glasses and a bottle.

The ghost sniffed several times. "Wonderful. I wish I could partake. Being dead has its disadvantages."

"Would it be all right if I sleep with you?" I ran to Simon's side and grabbed his arm. Maybe the ghost couldn't follow me there.

"You know those stairs wreak havoc on my arthritis," Simon said. "Calm down. It's only a bad dream."

"No." I stared at the smirking ghost. "I mean sleep in your room—with you."

"Miss Wellman!" Simon handed me a glass with a shot of whiskey in it. "I thought we had an understanding that this was only a professional relationship, even though we are living in the same house."

The ghost started laughing—big belly rolls that projected him across the ceiling.

"That's not what I meant. Really. I was hoping the

ghost couldn't go into the basement."

"Drink your whiskey, and you'll feel much better," Simon instructed. "Sleep here on the sofa if it makes you feel better. Try to get control of your emotions."

I drank the whiskey and watched as Simon took his cavalry sword and went back to the basement, locking the door from the kitchen behind him.

What could I do but hope the ghost went away? I sat with Wordsworth on my lap since the cats wouldn't come near. The ghost returned to the floor to contemplate me.

"I'm having a deuce of a time trying to understand why I'm here," he confessed as he strode back and forth across the Persian carpet. "Perhaps it's because they have desecrated my work, and it has pulled me from the grave for vengeance."

"If that's the case, surely you would have come back much sooner." I went back to the liquor cabinet and poured myself another whiskey. "I think plays have been performed of your work for more than a hundred years."

He screwed up his face. "More than—what date is it anyway?"

"2015." I took another sip, hoping if I drank enough that he'd vanish.

"Two thousand and fifteen, you say? That's absurd. The way the human race was carrying on in my time, it could never have lasted this long."

"I'm sorry. We managed. Now if you're done checking the date, will you please go away?"

"Does it not concern you, young woman, that I am here for a purpose? A spirit does not simply leave his grave with no idea of what to do."

"No, it doesn't concern me."

"Well, it concerns me. Perhaps I have been summoned to work on your redemption."

"I don't need to be redeemed, thank you." An idea hit me. "Did you visit here once? I don't know everything about your life, if you really are Charles Dickens. Maybe you stayed here, like George Washington, and now you're drawn back here."

He seemed to consider the matter. "Where are we?"

"Portsmouth."

"I say! I believe you hit the nail on the head. I was born in Portsmouth. It all makes sense now. If you are also from here, you might be one of my descendants. In that case, the drivel you're writing is even worse than I thought."

"No." That couldn't be right. "This isn't England. I think you were born in England."

"You said Portsmouth."

"Portsmouth, Virginia. Not Portsmouth, England."

"We're in the Colonies then, is that correct?"

"Yes. I'm sorry."

"Don't be. I'm much relieved. I was heartbroken that any descendant of mine could be so vapid and romantic. But I am still of the opinion that I am here to help with your writing. I have never been in this place so would have no purpose to come here other than responding to a suffering writer's call for help."

I swallowed the rest of the whiskey and accidentally dropped the glass. It rolled on the carpet without breaking. I started to pick it up but was too dizzy to lean over. I ended up falling back on the sofa and closing my eyes against the ghost's inquisitive face.

"There's no way I would have asked you for help," I mumbled, half asleep. "Maybe Jane Austen or Mary Shelley. But not you."

"We'll see about that," he retorted. "If nothing else, perhaps I can teach you how to hold your whiskey."

I fell asleep after his last words. I wanted to respond, but the words wouldn't come. It was just as well, my final thoughts reminded me. When I woke up again, it would be morning, and the ghost would be gone.

I hate it when I'm wrong.

Chapter Eight

Asking for Help

"I can never close my lips where I have opened my heart."

It was morning when I awoke. November sunlight streamed through the downstairs windows. Both cats were asleep on top of me. Wordsworth was attacking my feet as he looked for his breakfast. My mouth tasted like garbage, and my head pounded.

A brisk knock at the front door was followed by several rings of the bell. I tried to move, but the cats had dug their claws in. I heard Simon coming up from the basement.

I was still in my pajamas—nothing shocking or shameful, just shorts and a tank top. I could've answered the door but really wanted to run upstairs and go back to sleep. I slunk past the closed front door after another round of bell-ringing and pounding. The caller couldn't see me as I headed up the stairs.

"I'm coming," Simon said, not seeing me either.

By the time he was talking to whoever was at the door, I was back upstairs and snuggled into my bed. With any luck, no one would need me or even think about me being here for an hour or two.

Wishful thinking.

Footsteps came up the stairs to the second floor. I pulled the blanket over my head. The tapping sound of hard-soled shoes climbing the spiral staircase followed rapidly. I groaned as the door to my bedroom opened, and I pretended to be asleep.

"You know I could see you on the sofa when I came up the walk," Daniel said. "You need a shade or something if you're going to sleep there."

"Go away. I'm sick."

"Too bad. I need your help."

I peeked out from under the blanket. His face was unpleasantly fuzzy. I was still suffering from the effects of last night's bout with whiskey. "What for?"

"I could use some background into the life of Simon Canterville."

Even though my head still throbbed, I sat up and glared at him. He was much closer than I'd expected—sitting on the edge of the bed. When had he made that move? It was my own fault for not looking. I should've known I had to keep an eye on him.

"I thought you were done with him? Did the

French dueling pistol match the one that shot Mr. Hart?"

"I don't know, but doesn't it bother you that your partner could still be held responsible for the murder if anything happens to tip the scale? Where's all that fire from yesterday? I remember you saying you'd do anything to help him."

Was it me, or did I hear laughter float through the bedroom on a cool breeze?

I shivered and pulled the blanket up to my chin.

Daniel laughed. "Too late to be modest, Lisa."

"That was a long time ago." I tried not to let his comment rankle, but it did. I didn't know if there was enough time that could pass between us that his remarks wouldn't bother me. "You don't want my help. Get off my bed and leave."

His eyes were as warm and caring as I'd remembered when he said, "I'm only asking you for help because I don't think the old guy did it. If you work with me, it might be easier to prove it. He's not very open as far as giving information I can use to find the killer and get him out of this mess."

"Why do you want to help him?" I studied his face through narrowed eyes, refusing to be drawn into whatever was going on.

He shrugged and got up. "I'm involved, and I don't want the wrong person in jail. Do you want to help or not?"

"You know I do."

Daniel paced around the room, picking up my things and looking at them before putting them back. "Hart had a strong case against opening the book shop here, according to the people I've talked to. He might not have been able to keep the shop from opening forever, but he was making it take longer and cost a lot more. Canterville applied for his business license last year."

"He wasn't keeping him from opening the book shop. There are other examples of businesses in Olde Town outside of the main business area. Look at the Mermaid Bed and Breakfast. And there are lawyers and psychologists who practice here. Simon would've won no matter what."

I didn't know that, but I knew Simon owned the house and had plenty of start-up capital. He was also a patient man. He was confident that he'd win in the long run.

"I don't see how I can be of much help." I shifted in bed, wishing he'd leave.

"Why are you here?" He significantly glanced around the room. "Last time I checked, you were still living with your mother and working at the library."

He'd checked up on me? I should've been angry, I supposed, but instead I felt that little surge of happiness that I'd always felt with him. That was twelve years ago, I reminded myself, squishing down hard on that little surge as though it was a nasty bug.

"I can't believe you were checking on me." I feigned anger. It was the easiest emotion to deal with when it came to Daniel. "That's called stalking, in case you didn't know."

"Can't a man notice what's going on in his ex-wife's life? I just saw your name and wondered what you were doing." He shrugged. "It's not like we ever hated each other, Lisa. We just kind of drifted apart."

Oh. I really hated it when he looked at me that

way.

"So you decided to pull all my cell phone records and check my bank account."

"What? No. That's not what I said."

That was it. I had to get out of the bed. I grabbed my robe as I got up, conscious of his gaze on me. I needed to start sleeping in sweat pants and a big shirt for times like this. Not sure how many of those there would be, but this one had taught me a valuable lesson.

"All right. I'll do whatever you need me to do to help Simon. But get out of my room so I can get dressed."

Daniel grinned, flashing that fabulous smile at me. "That's more like it. I'll wait for you downstairs."

"What a delightful conundrum!" Dickens laughed as he appeared.

I grabbed the chair at my desk and held it in front of me as I pressed myself against the wall.

He was real. I hadn't dreamed him. Or I was crazy, though it didn't run in my family. Either way, there he was again. I didn't even believe in ghosts. But it didn't matter to my racing heart and trembling hands.

"My dear young woman, the man is in love with you. Do you feel the same about him?"

"No, I don't love him. Not anymore. He doesn't love me either. It's just the way men talk."

"As a man and an astute observer of the human condition, I tell you that man is in love with you." He played with a large ring on his finger. "That you do not feel the same is good. A serious writer doesn't have time for such things. We must be of the world, not in it. Dispassionate observation is the key. It is difficult to fully participate when one is in the throes of passion or any other strong emotion."

I'd always heard that Dickens was wordy and enjoyed hearing himself speak. History was correct on that.

What was I saying? This wasn't Charles Dickens. It wasn't Barry either. I could see that now. It was some kind of trick or a prank. I didn't know how it was being done, but I planned to find out. Until then, I'd go along with it.

"What do you want? Is there something that you left undone and need me to finish for you?" It seemed unlikely since he'd been dead a long time. I seriously hoped he didn't have a manuscript he wanted to dictate to me from beyond. His work did well in his day, but I wasn't sure how it would sell in my century. Still, everyone had a story.

"Of course not. Not that I would entrust such a thing to you—a woman I barely know. I told you why I have come. Your pathetic lamentations as an author touched my heart and drew me here to be of assistance."

"That's kind of you but—"

"Kindness had nothing to do with it. Even in my present state, I can feel pain. Your writing is painful to me." He rubbed his hands together. "And now it seems I am also part of a mystery. How wonderful. There is nothing I love above solving other people's problems."

I sat in my chair, my head in my hands. It had been easy to get Daniel out the door. Dickens, or whoever he was, was more determined to stay.

"Fine. You can help me write my book and figure out who killed Ebenezer Hart. But go away while I get dressed. If I don't get some tea soon, my head is going to fall off."

"Ebenezer, you say?" His hand went to his chin.

"Apt, that, eh? One of my greatest creations, Ebenezer Scrooge. Even trying to emulate him now. I always knew I'd be immortal, if in word rather than in flesh."

"Speaking of flesh, I need to get dressed so I can go downstairs. Would you mind leaving?"

He cleared his throat. "Did you truly believe Charles Dickens would watch a woman unknown to him change her attire? I have always been a gentleman!"

And he vanished. I didn't know if that meant he was actually gone or I just couldn't see him. I took my clothes into the bathroom and changed in there with the lights off. What was I doing? Why was this happening to me? That couldn't be Charles Dickens—not even the ghost of Charles Dickens. So what was going on?

I had an idea how to get those answers. A friend of mine in the writer's group, Dana Whitley, wrote paranormal fiction as a spinoff from her day job as a parapsychologist. She might have some answers, but I was going to have to wait until tomorrow to see her.

In the meantime, I'd have to handle Dickens, or whatever it was, the best I could.

Chapter Nine

A Friendly Exchange

"There are strings in the human heart that had better not be vibrated."

When I got out of the bathroom, I glanced both ways, but there was no sign of Dickens. I shoved my feet into boots and caught a glance of myself in the antique mirror by the door. My hair looked better tied back with a green ribbon that matched my shirt. I put on a little lipstick. I also lied to myself when I thought it was only because I'd have to deal with people about the book shop — not because Daniel was there.

Truffles and Maggie May waited patiently for me

to go downstairs and feed them. I didn't see Puck anywhere, but that wasn't unusual. He declared his independence and unwillingness to conform by making me find him.

I heard Simon talking to Daniel and smelled food cooking. Wordsworth was still by the door, huffing out his tiny bark to let us know that someone had come inside that didn't belong there.

"There she is!" Simon called out when he saw me. "And looking beautiful today. Are you going out, Lisa? You usually don't dress up when you're planning on only being around the house."

It was too late to wish he wouldn't have pointed that out to Daniel. I didn't want him to get the idea that I might have dressed up for him. It certainly wasn't true.

"There are a few errands I need to run." I mentally scrambled to decide what those were.

"Lisa's agreed to help me with the case, Mr. Canterville," Daniel explained. "We still need to figure out who killed Mr. Hart and left him on your roof."

"Yes, of course. I can handle things today without her." Simon put fresh croissants on the table with a cow-shaped holder filled with softened butter. "Please have something to eat, Detective."

"He's not a detective anymore, strictly speaking," I explained as I made a fresh cup of tea. "He works directly for the chief of police. He'll probably be the next chief of police, like his father."

Daniel took a pastry. "Thank you, sir. They smell delicious. I don't know if I'll actually make it that far. Chief Masterson is barely fifty. He has a long time until retirement. We'll see how it goes."

"But all of Daniel's family is involved in some form of law enforcement," I said. "His sister, Linda, is an ADA. His mother is a judge. I think Chief Masterson will make room for another member of the Fairhaven family."

It was a little snarky. Okay—it was really snarky. But Daniel's family had a lot to do with us breaking up. His wife needed to be someone who could fit in with them and stand near whatever podium Daniel was speaking from, while gazing respectfully at him.

Funny how I hadn't thought about it in years, but only a few minutes with Daniel reminded me of how angry and incompetent they'd made me feel. A librarian in their family? The least I could be was a lawyer.

"Just because members of my family have taken the path of civil service doesn't mean we're evil overlords or something." Daniel actually seemed embarrassed. He took a sip of his coffee and darted an angry glance my way. "These croissants are delicious, sir. I hope your cooking skills are rubbing off on Lisa."

Simon's eyes slowly swiveled between Daniel and me as he sat down. "I assume the two of you know one another. I'm getting that impression. Perhaps I'm mistaken."

"No." I added extra sugar to my tea. "You're correct. Daniel and I have known each other since college."

I didn't want to go into it any deeper. We'd only been married for six months twelve years ago. There was nothing more to say.

"Actually, we were married." Daniel glanced up and smiled as though he knew I hadn't wanted to talk about it.

"Married?" Simon's white brows shot up at the words. "You never mentioned it, Miss Wellman. A failure to report your marital status can be a grievous error."

"We haven't been married for twelve years," I explained through clenched teeth. Daniel was having fun with this. "I would've mentioned it if it had been important. We were only married a short time, and I rarely even think of it. I didn't mean to sound deceitful."

"That's quite all right," Simon said. "I myself had a brief fling with a British nurse in Hawaii once. We never married. The one marriage I had to my beloved Ariadne was the only commitment I was ever willing to make to a woman—until you—Miss Wellman. And of course, I hadn't mentioned my son to you either."

Daniel nearly choked on his coffee. I gave him several more cloth napkins, and Simon patted him heartily on the back. I knew what he was thinking, and I wasn't in any hurry to correct his thoughts. It served him right for sneaking up on me the way he had.

"Thank you, Simon." I looked lovingly at him. "You certainly changed my life too."

We finished breakfast, and I knew the end of my charade was coming. Funny how Daniel and I had only known each other well for a short time so long ago, and yet I could still read his thoughts written clearly on his handsome face.

"I'd best get moving on the new books." Simon got to his feet. "A wonderful task, going through books old and new. I can't believe any other profession to be superior to mine."

Daniel and I helped clear the table and tidy the kitchen. The cats had finished eating and were lounging around the kitchen, grooming themselves. Wordsworth looked for a tidbit from breakfast, which Simon gladly gave him as he laughed at his tricks.

"If you're ready, Lisa," Daniel said. "I thought we'd go to my office to look over that information."

"Yes. I'm ready. I'll be back in a few hours," I promised Simon. I didn't want him to fret over the idea that the police were still investigating him. He had certain ideas about honor and doing what was right in life. I knew we could figure out who was responsible for Mr. Hart's death without making him feel as though he was still in the crosshairs.

"Excellent, my dear." He was already opening a box of newer books. "And just who is this Mary Higgins Clark, and should I be reading her books?"

I laughed and informed him that she was a well-known mystery writer. "You should definitely read some of her work."

There was no way to put it off any longer. I left the house with Daniel and got in his car.

He immediately turned to me. "You didn't tell me you were romantically involved with Canterville. Maybe you can't be much help after all."

"I knew you were thinking that." I enjoyed telling him. "Simon and I are just friends and business associates. And not the kind of friends you are with Francine Parker."

I saw the smile grow on his face before I realized that I'd overplayed my hand.

"So you've been keeping up with me too." He grinned as he started the car. "That's nice to know."

"Unlike you going out of your way to find out what was happening in my life, I can't pick up a newspaper or listen to TV without seeing you and Francine together at some charity event or other. You're the talk of the town. And don't bother telling me that the two of you are only friends."

"Francine is going through a bad divorce right now," he said. "In her position, she needs someone to go places with her. And it keeps everyone from asking who I'm dating."

He drove around the block to a coffeehouse that I usually walked to when I wanted to get out of the house. "I thought we'd talk here."

"I don't know what you're looking for from me." Being with him made me feel more defensive than I would have if it had been some unknown police detective.

"Like I said, I'm missing some key parts to the whole feud between Hart and your boyfriend."

"Not my boyfriend."

"Okay. Your boss."

"Not my boss. I don't work for Simon."

"All right. Why don't you tell me what you do for Canterville?" His tone was laced with sarcasm that probably wouldn't have been there if he hadn't been talking to me.

"Simon and I are partners in the Canterville Book Shop. He has the money and a place for the shop. I know a lot about books and running the business part of it."

"You always talked about book shops." He smiled briefly. "I guess I thought you'd be happy being a librarian."

"I was." I was surprised that he remembered all those rambling conversations we'd had so long ago. "I needed a change."

"So you gave up your job at the library and moved in with him. Why not stay at your place with your mother and run the business from there? What does she think of the idea?"

I swallowed hard on the pain his words brought me. Of course he'd know about everything but this. "My mother died last month. I had to sell the house to pay for her medical bills."

"I didn't know." He immediately put his warm hand on mine. "I'm so sorry, Lisa."

"I was living with Liz when this came up. She has four kids now. Not much privacy. This way I work on the book shop during the day, and I have time at night to work on my manuscript."

His eyes got wide. "You're really writing? I thought you were joking. Not many people get to do what they dream about. Congratulations."

To get past my slight tendency to weepiness regarding my mother's passing and Daniel's unexpected acceptance of the choices I'd made, I cleared my throat and glanced out the window. "Are we going inside or just sitting here in the car?"

"No. Let's go in."

"Good."

He ordered tea for me and coffee for him. We sat in a corner booth in the back of the shop. I let him pay for our drinks and bring them to the table. I figured this meeting was on him anyway, since he'd asked for my help.

When we were settled, I started to think about his

line of questioning in the car. It was personal and had nothing to do with the murder he was supposed to be investigating.

"What exactly are you looking for from me, Daniel? Everything you've asked me so far has been about my life and nothing to do with Simon or Mr. Hart's death. How about giving me a straight answer?"

I could see he was collecting his thoughts. I remembered that about him too. Daniel didn't like to answer without thinking about what he was going to say.

"Your background information goes to understanding Simon's frame of mind," he finally said. "You told me that he wasn't desperate or impatient to open the book shop—a reason that he might kill Mr. Hart."

"But he's not stupid either. He wouldn't dump the body on the roof. No one would who wasn't trying to frame him for murder."

"That might be true, but I've seen people do a lot of stupid things, Lisa. Somehow they always think they're going to get away with it."

"Well, it wasn't Simon. I do have an idea of someone you should look into—his son, Ashcroft. I met him for the first time yesterday. They aren't close, but when Ashcroft thought Simon was going to prison, he came right over to claim his house and everything else."

"There's still the problem about how Mr. Hart got on the roof without you hearing anything." He studied me after writing down Ashcroft's name. "Any ideas on that?"

"Do you think I killed Mr. Hart and dumped him

out of my window? Is that what all the personal questions were about?"

"No, of course not. Like I said, just getting some insight from you on what happened."

I sipped my tea. Daniel had never been a good liar, and I didn't think he was lying about me being a suspect. "Let's say he wasn't dumped out of my window. There are other ways he could get up there. Maybe someone pulled him up with a rope. Have you checked for rope fibers on the shingles?"

"That's pretty creative. I take it you're writing murder mysteries."

"What does that mean? I've sat through seminars with law enforcement from the FBI and CIA to the Secret Service and local police. What may sound creative might be exactly what happened. What about shoe prints in the yard around the house? Did you do any plaster casts so we could check for shoe sizes and types?"

He sat back in his chair. "No. Nothing like that because the working theory is that he was shoved out your window."

"Well maybe you should take a fresh look and break through your working-theory rut."

"Maybe so." He finished his coffee. "Are you sure about Simon's finances? Have you actually seen his bank statements or checked his credit? He might not be as well-off as you think."

"No." I had to admit I hadn't thought to question Simon after seeing his house and the hundreds of thousands of dollars in antiques that were carelessly scattered inside. "I guess we both have something to look into. Will you check the shingles for fibers and the yard for shoe prints?"

"I will—if you'll verify his finances for me."

That made me suspicious. "I know you can get a warrant to check his bank and credit. Why do you want me to do it?"

"It would be less work than if I have to get a court order."

He'd had to think about it. I knew he was lying. But why would he lie about such an obvious thing?

"All right. I said I'd help. I'll check his bank statement and credit, but I think you'll find he's everything that he seems." This seemed to be the best way to play this until I could find out what was really going on.

"Mind if I ask how you teamed up with him?"

"Not at all. He came into the library almost every day for a few years. I think he's read every book there. He started telling me about opening the book shop. The more I heard, the more I wanted to be part of it. It's exciting. I can't wait until it opens."

"Yeah. I guess you'd feel that way. Just wondering." Daniel got to his feet and took our cups to the counter. "That should do it for now. You have my cell number so you can call when you have that information. I'll send someone over to check on the footprints."

"And the rope fibers," I reminded him.

"That too." He smiled. "Thanks for your help, Lisa. And again, I'm sorry about your mother. I know she hated me, but I really liked her."

"She didn't hate you. She was just afraid that what happened would happen. She was a big believer in knowing her place and not moving out of it."

"You don't really believe that we didn't work because of my family, do you?"

"I don't know." I took a deep breath. "It was a long time ago. I haven't thought about it in years. I'll just walk back to the house from here. See you later."

I could feel his eyes on me as I left the coffee shop. They made me remember all the sadness that had come with our break up.

The morning had gotten colder, and I was sorry I hadn't worn a coat as I passed a few people walking their dogs and watched one man putting up a family of snow people in his yard. "O Little Town of Bethlehem" was coming from the old stone church on the corner. The door and walkway leading up to it were artfully decorated with hundreds of poinsettias.

It didn't feel like Thanksgiving or Christmas was coming, even though all the signs were there. Maybe I was too focused on the book shop, or maybe I was dreading the first Christmas without my mother. Whatever it was, I wasn't in the holiday spirit as I should have been. A murder, and the possible ghost of Charles Dickens haunting me, didn't help matters.

Chapter Ten

Death By Fear

"It was the best of time, it was the worst of times."

I was quiet going into the house, hoping that Dickens wouldn't hear me if he was still there. I glanced around the front foyer and up the wide stairs. Happily he was nowhere to be found.

Intent on finishing my distasteful job of looking into Simon's personal finances, I turned toward the kitchen and all but jumped out of my skin. Dickens had been standing right behind me.

"Are you trying to kill me?" I demanded angrily. "You could give someone a heart attack like that."

"Hmm," he considered, shaggy brows knit together. "Death by fear. A great title for a novel—if you had one. Where have you been? I thought you were serious about your craft. God save me! I was brought back to aid a dilettante writer."

I thought about Simon using that term for Mrs. Tappen, and it made me laugh. "I'd like to write all the time, but there are other aspects of life that must be taken care of."

"Are you laughing at me? Do you find me humorous? I admit to enjoying it when critics call me satirical, but I refuse to be outright laughed at. Summon me when you plan to take your muse seriously."

He vanished, and I slumped against the banister. It was hardly ten a.m., and it had already been that kind of day. I went to find Simon and ask for his financial records. Daniel didn't say that he couldn't know what I was doing. I was his friend. I didn't plan to spy on him, whether it made it easier for Daniel or not.

"Simon?" I looked through the kitchen and two of the parlors. I could see he'd been there, adding books to shelves and leaving boxes with books in them. We'd had the idea of having different categories of books in each room and naming the rooms for them.

I couldn't find him anywhere and finally went downstairs calling his name so he'd know I was coming in case he was changing clothes or something personal. He'd been careful to respect my privacy, and I did the same for him. "Simon? Are you down here?"

The basement was the size of the house and fitted elegantly with paneled walls and nice carpet underfoot. Simon knew how to live and indulged himself with niceties. He'd indulged me too, even though my space was much smaller. Still I had the wonderful turret room. How could I ask for a better place to write?

I found him asleep on a sofa. He must have exhausted himself. I smiled at his face and imagined how handsome he must've been when he was young. He'd described himself in his youth as a rakehell who courted many beautiful women. I believed him.

"Simon?" I shook him a little, but there was no response. I called his name again, starting to panic. When I grabbed his hand, it was icy and clammy. There was a faint, blue smudge around his mouth, and his breathing was labored. "Simon!"

Trying to remember what I was supposed to do at this point—I'd had dozens of CPR classes and other emergency seminars at writer's workshops—I did what I knew I should do and dialed 911. Then I called Daniel. What if Simon had been poisoned and using CPR on him made the poison work faster?

"Did you call emergency services?" Daniel asked. "I'll be there as soon as I can."

"Okay. I won't touch anything."

"He's probably had a heart attack or stroke."

"Or he's been poisoned because killing Mr. Hart didn't do what the killer wanted." I heard the EMS at the front door and hung up. "We're down here," I yelled for them. "Hurry, please."

The EMS techs got Simon on a stretcher after failing to revive him. He was breathing, but it was shallow, and his heartbeat was slow and irregular.

Daniel arrived as I was starting to search the room. I knew I should've looked before the EMS arrived, but it was all I could do to hold Simon's hand and encourage him to stay alive.

"Are you okay?" he asked. "What are you doing? You don't have to look for his financial records now. You should be with him."

"That's not what I'm looking for." I didn't stop moving dozens of throw pillows out of the way. Simon had a thing for throw pillows. "I wanted to make sure no one left any clues that we could use to save him. It's always better if you know what kind of poison was used."

"You don't know that he was poisoned."

"And you don't know that he wasn't." I paused. "You know, there was a faint scent about him that wasn't normal. It wasn't something ordinary like almonds. That would've been easy."

He put his hands on my arms and stared into my face. "Just because you read about this stuff doesn't make it real. People just don't go around randomly poisoning people much anymore. I've never worked a case that involved poison. Let me take you to the hospital so you can be with him."

Tears were caught in my throat, and I couldn't respond. He wrapped his arms around me and held me close. I wanted to push him away, but I couldn't. I was glad he was there.

And then I spotted it—a small, brown bottle tipped on its side on the floor. I grabbed the handkerchief out of Daniel's pocket and used it to pick up the bottle in case there were fingerprints on it.

"What is it?" he asked in a disbelieving voice.

"Lavender oil. I knew there was something unusual. Simon hates the smell of lavender, and the oil is a poison if ingested." I held up the bottle. "There's nothing in it, and you can see the seal was improperly broken in the killer's haste to administer it to Simon. Call the hospital. Let them know that he's been poisoned."

"All right." He scanned the bottle and replied in a stunned voice. "I'll let them know, but we'd better hurry to get the bottle to the hospital so they know how to treat him."

"Activated charcoal and gastric lavage," I replied in a certain, if scared voice. "Wait. We might need his information." I grabbed the folder he kept in his roll-top desk that included his Social Security number and insurance information.

He finished talking to the doctor at the hospital and grabbed my hand. "Let's go. I don't think the doctor was convinced. He may need to see the bottle."

We ran upstairs, and I locked the door, wishing I could also set the alarm to keep Ashcroft out. I had to talk to Simon about an alarm as soon as he was well. He had to be well again. I closed my eyes and prayed but was not as convinced of its efficacy after my mother's death. I'd prayed a lot while she was sick, but those prayers had never been answered. A cold fear for Simon clutched at my heart, but I didn't tell Daniel as we drove quickly with the siren on to the hospital.

The chief of the emergency room met us at the door. Daniel gave him the brown bottle. He sniffed it and stared at us. "Are you poison experts or something?"

"No, sir." Daniel showed him his badge. "We have knowledge of the victim that leads us to believe he may have been poisoned with lavender oil."

"What kind of knowledge?" The doctor's brow

furrowed in disbelief.

"I know the victim, Mr. Simon Canterville, Dr. Brown." I glanced at his nametag and then into his face. "Mr. Canterville hates the smell of lavender and wouldn't have it in his room or on his person. I believe he may have been tricked into swallowing it in his tea."

"And you are?"

"Lisa Wellman. I live with Simon Canterville."

"Look," he hesitated. "I'm sure you mean well, young woman, but I've been a doctor for many years and have never seen a malicious case of poisoning."

"I'm going to the media if you don't start working on Mr. Canterville. I've given you the information you need. I think you know what to do. If not, I can tell you how to treat lavender poisoning."

Dr. Brown continued to have a stunned, deer-in-the-headlights expression on his face. He was about to say something else when a nurse came to get him.

"It appears the tip you received about the poisoning was accurate, Doctor," she said. "Should we begin gastric lavage now?"

He conferred with her for a moment before curtly nodding at us and going back down the hall.

"I hate to sound stupid, but what's gastric lavage?" Daniel asked me.

"Stomach pumping." I'd been right. The knowledge made my knees weak and I dropped into a chair. "Oh, my God. Someone tried to kill Simon."

"Let me get you some water. Sometimes it just hits you like that."

I thought, *really* thought, about what this meant. It was one thing to react on gut instinct about what had happened and another to realize that someone Simon knew and trusted had actually tried to kill him. What was going on?

By the time Daniel had returned with a weak cup of tea, I was full of questions. "Why would anyone want to kill Simon?"

He sat beside me. "I'm assuming it has something to do with the dead man on the roof. What did you say his son's name is?"

"Ashcroft. I guess his last name is the same. I don't know where he lives or much about him."

"And yet you accused him of murder and attempted murder," Daniel reminded me as he texted on his phone. "I'm having someone look him up and bring him in for questioning. We can at least find out where he was when Mr. Hart was killed and when someone poisoned his father."

"But how do these things go together? Was he really so impatient to get at Simon's money that he couldn't wait to see if he'd be charged with murder and go to prison?"

He smiled. "I think I may have to hire you, Lisa. You're better at asking questions than I am."

"I'm just thinking about the story." I got up and paced the floor. "Simon has money and a feud with Mr. Hart about the bookshop. Ashcroft sees his inheritance going down the tubes if he doesn't act. He kills Simon's frenemy to make him look guilty."

"Frenemy?"

"Yes. They used to be friends, but they had a serious falling out years ago—so now enemies. They've butted heads in the past, but this was the biggest problem of all."

"I'll keep that term in mind." Daniel checked his

phone when he received a text. "I've got Ashcroft's address. I'm going out there to pick him up, if you'll be okay."

"Thanks, but I've been okay on my own for a long time. Just figure out if Ashcroft is responsible for this. I'm going to shop for a security company while I wait to hear about Simon."

"Yeah. Sorry." He scratched his head. "I didn't mean to sound like you needed me hanging around or anything. I'll see you later. Keep me posted about Simon. Good call on the poison."

I sat down in the uncomfortable, plastic chair when Daniel was gone. I tried to concentrate on some emails about books being shipped to us and ended up looking over security companies online. It seemed to take forever to hear from the doctor. But that's the way it always was waiting for information about someone you cared for.

Two security firms that had good references and weren't too far away from Olde Town. I bookmarked them, though it wouldn't have made any difference to what happened to Simon. It was clear he trusted whoever gave him the poison. But it might have prevented the whole mess with Mr. Hart. How much would it cost to have twenty-four-hour videotaping inside and outside the house?

Chapter Eleven

The Search for Answers

"I would gladly think otherwise if I could."

"That much?" I couldn't believe it was that expensive to set up a camera and twenty-four-hour feed with recording. "Well, how much is it just to get security on the house?"

That was more reasonable. "All right. Thanks. Let me talk to my partner and get back with you. What did you say your name was?"

Dr. Brown was standing in front of me as I ended the conversation with the security man. "Miss Wellman, I believe?"

"Yes." I nervously got to my feet. "How is he?"

"Very well. He's in remarkably good shape for a man his age." He glanced around the empty waiting area. "Is there no family I should be speaking to?"

"No." I lied, but it was only to protect Simon from his possibly evil son. "I'm as close to a family as Mr. Canterville has. May I see him?"

"For a few minutes. He needs his rest."

"Do you have an ETA on when you expect him to be released?"

"Probably tomorrow if things go well," Dr. Brown assured me.

"Thank you. That's good news. What room is he in?"

"The nurse at the desk over there can tell you. She also has paperwork that needs to be filled out. May I ask how you came to be so knowledgeable in detecting poison? It's not something that happens often."

"Of course. I've been to dozens of workshops and seminars given by the CDC and Poison Control. It's important for a mystery writer to know signs and symptoms of poisoning."

"A mystery writer? I thought perhaps you were an actual expert in the field."

"No, not really. But I'm good at noticing things that don't seem right. Like the smell of lavender in Mr. Canterville's room. Thank you, Dr. Brown. I'm sorry if I was harsh with you, but every moment counts when it comes to counteracting poison, don't you agree?"

"Yes, of course." He seemed bewildered. "Nice to meet you, Miss Wellman."

I left him to go to the nurse's station and fill out the paperwork. I wanted to see Simon as soon as possible.

It still took over an hour before the nurse gave me his room number and pointed to the elevator. I didn't think I'd ever be done with answering questions for her. The hardest one for her to accept was that Simon didn't regularly take prescription drugs.

"He swims three times a week at the Y," I told her. "And he takes vitamins."

She stared at me a moment as though I'd lost my mind. "Uh huh. Are you sure?"

After I'd assured her a dozen times, she finally wrote it down on his chart. I was happy to finally get away from her.

Simon was awake and trying to use the remote for the TV. He smiled when he saw me. "Miss Wellman. I can't tell you how good it is to see you. Perhaps you can work this blasted thing."

I switched off the TV and took his hand. "I'm so glad you're all right. I was worried about you."

"Pish posh. No need to worry. I've been through worse. That year with malaria burning through my body was one of those times. I knew the villages in India were rife with it, but it had been important to deliver the supplies to the doctors there. I was finally cured by a holy man in Pakistan. Bright old chap. Made a tolerable cup of tea."

He still looked pale and fragile lying in the hospital bed wearing a blue paper gown that crackled as he moved.

"You're okay. That's what matters. What happened? Who tricked you into swallowing the lavender?"

"Lavender? I didn't have lavender. Hate the stuff. You know that. What are you talking about?" He put his hand to my forehead. "You are slightly feverish. Perhaps we should change places. I feel fine."

"All right." I took a step back in the conversation. "I found you unconscious on the sofa in your room. There was an empty bottle of lavender oil on the floor. There may have been some in your tea. Who gave you the tea?"

He still looked confused. "I did not take tea after you left. I was busy working until I went to my room after hearing an unusual sound. I thought perhaps we had bats."

"Bats?"

"You know—winged rats." He waved his arms a few times to mimic flying.

"What? Are you sure you're all right, Simon? You drank lavender oil. That's why you're here." Could this be a side effect of the poison? Maybe he really had no idea what happened.

"Positively." He frowned as he thought about that morning. "I didn't see anything, but I felt a slight bump and was a trifle woozy for a moment. I sat on the sofa and woke up here with some man peering into my eyes with a bright light."

"A bump? Sit up and let me take a look at your head."

Sure enough, there was a small bump on the back of his head. It didn't appear to have broken the skin, but it must have been enough to daze him. While he was nearly unconscious, the killer had poured the lavender into his throat. It was heinous, to be sure.

"You might have to go through a few more tests to make sure you don't have a concussion," I told him. "I'm sorry. I was so sure you'd taken the lavender with your tea."

"Good heavens, Miss Wellman! How would I get that cup close to my face with that obnoxious smell?"

"You're right. I'll speak with your doctor and be back later."

He sighed heavily. "Very well."

"One more thing. I think we should consider a security system for the house. I don't know how much money you want to put into it, but nearly all businesses have one now."

Simon raised his brows. "Is Wordsworth not enough?"

"No. I'm sorry." I kissed his forehead. "We had a dead man on the roof, and someone poisoned you. Not to mention other instances that could have been avoided with a security system."

"All right. Do what you think is best. I rely on your judgment." He smiled slyly. "But not even Wordsworth or your much-vaunted security system could have kept young detective Fairhaven from your boudoir this morning. I believe he has what they call the 'hots' for you, in today's vernacular."

"Yeah. We'll talk about that when you get home. I'll be back in a little while."

I spoke with Dr. Brown on my way out of the hospital. It seemed he'd already noticed the bump on Simon's head and had planned to talk to him about it. He wasn't scheduling any other tests unless Simon's condition improved.

"But as a poison expert, you should know that straight lavender oil would have burned his throat. It had to be diluted with something. And then it wasn't the entire 15ml that the bottle contained, or we might not have been able to save him without extreme liver damage."

It gave me something to think about. It was possible that Ashcroft only had a partial bottle of lavender oil. Or he hadn't meant to kill Simon, only scare him.

"Could I get that bottle back that we gave you? There may be fingerprints on it that we can use."

"Deputy Chief Fairhaven took it with him. Maybe he could have it checked."

I agreed with him and went out to the curb to hail a taxi. Whether it was Ashcroft or someone else, so many attacks so close were beginning to scare me. I gave the driver the address and kind of wished I had somewhere else to go. I'd thrown in my lot with Simon very quickly, not looking before I leaped.

It had just been such a perfect opportunity for me to do something I'd always wanted and at a time that I'd needed the distraction. It'd made sense for me to give up everything to live with Simon and get the book shop set up.

Now I wasn't so sure.

Daniel called as I was getting out of the taxi. They'd located Ashcroft and taken him into the station for questioning. "But right now, it sounds like he might have a good alibi for Mr. Hart's death and the attack on Simon. What did you get on your end?"

"I found a lump on the back of Simon's head." I told him my revised theory on what had happened. "The doctor said the lavender oil wasn't strong enough to kill him, just make him sick. Simon doesn't remember any of it. He's no help at all discovering who did this to him."

"That's too bad and still leaves us with the problem of making sure he doesn't get blamed for Mr. Hart's death."

"But someone tried to poison him. Isn't that enough proof that he's not guilty? There could be a conspiracy."

"Since he could have given himself a low dose of lavender oil, what happened to him doesn't count, Lisa. We're back to square one where you look up his financial records for me. Is that still possible?"

"Yes." I grunted my disapproval. "But I think it's wrong. Have you had someone check the roof and the ground around the house?"

"No. I have a request for a crime scene tech to go out there, but they've been busy. Don't worry. It'll happen. You just watch your back until we know what's going on."

"Yeah. Sure." I hung up and went inside. I was glad the door wasn't open. Wordsworth and all three cats were in the foyer watching the door. I thought they'd probably be following someone around if something was wrong.

I wasn't happy knowing that someone could be in there waiting for me. Not that I had any money or anything else that someone would be interested in. I finally decided to sit on the stairs and call the security firm that had sounded best. I was in luck, and they offered to send someone out right away to install it.

While I was at it, I called my writing friend, Dana, to ask if she was busy with anything that evening. We weren't meeting with the group until the following night, but I thought I could really use her help with my other problem—Dickens.

"I'd love to come over and help you look for ghosts," she said. "Let's plan about nine-thirty. Can I bring my team?"

"That's fine. Bring whoever can come. I don't think we'll have to look too hard for him. He kind of hams it up when he makes an appearance." I was carefully scanning the area around me as I spoke. There was no sign of him yet, but I didn't want to take any chances that he wasn't gone for good.

"Excellent. I've got some new toys I've been dying to play with. I can't write about them until I know how they work. See you later, Lisa."

I put my phone in my pocket and took a deep breath. I might as well get on with looking at Simon's financial records. Then Daniel could get off his back and search for the real killer.

Getting up to go back to the basement, I turned to the left, and there was Dickens, grinning like a Cheshire cat. I took a few steps back and tripped over Puck, which caused him to hiss at me and run away as I fell back against the stairs.

"By George, haunting is a capital amusement." He laughed down at me with his hands on his hips. "Is it time yet for you to work on your musings?"

I took a deep breath, trying to ignore the pain in my side where I'd hit the stairs. "No, I'm afraid not. I have things I have to do."

"Bah, humbug. Do you think I would have written so many books in my lifetime if I'd let every little thing divert my attention from the important matter of my work? Of course not. What could be so important now that you must stray from your desk? I swear you are as skittish as Bob Cratchit!"

"Oh, I don't know. Ebenezer Hart was killed and dropped on our roof. People think my partner may have killed him. But then today someone tried to kill my partner. Does that sound like a good reason?"

He rubbed his hands together. "It sounds like grain for the gristmill, my dear. Throw away that drivel — along with the mewling female who is alone and scared in a house — and embrace the gift the gods have thrown your way."

"I'm not abandoning April Fitzhugh," I told him as I started walking toward the basement where Simon kept everything. "I've already worked on that manuscript for two years. I'm not going to give up on it."

"Then you condemn yourself to mediocrity."

"Whatever. I'm busy right now. Maybe we can talk about my writing later." *After Dana comes to exorcize you.*

"You are squandering your gift."

Charles Dickens wasn't exactly my favorite author but if he really thought I was gifted — wow. I paused and stared at his less-than-solid form. "I have a gift? You think I have a gift?"

He pulled his arms behind his back and faced me squarely. "It looks as though you will never know. And this is why women should not write. Good day."

I'd walked right into that one. If there was one thing I'd learned about being a writer, it was never to seek approval from other, better-known writers. My group was different. We supported each other. But a few friends had gone to see famous writers who actually told them they shouldn't bother working on their manuscripts because they'd never be good enough.

Switching on the lights in Simon's bedroom, I knew
Dickens was one of those writers. I'd fallen for his line
saying I might be gifted. It wouldn't happen again,
especially since Dana and her crew would get rid of
him.

Simon kept all of his records handwritten and
neatly organized in a file cabinet by his desk. I felt
terrible looking through his things, like I was betraying
his trust. What had I been thinking? I should've made
Daniel get a court order to check out his records. Why
was I helping him anyway?

"Because this way Simon doesn't have to be
embarrassed about it," I told myself. But honestly, I
knew I'd fallen for a line from Daniel and the curse of
his big, blue eyes.

"But no damage done," I advised myself. "Nothing
that can't be covered up with a smile anyway. My heart
isn't involved. Not again. Not this time."

I found what Daniel wanted and made copies of it.
Simon was much better off than even I'd guessed. He
owned several other properties in Olde Town that he
was renting. He wasn't hurting for money at all, as I'd
thought, and could have waited out anything Ebenezer
Hart could have thrown at him. I felt vindicated that I
was right about the money situation not being a reason
for Simon to kill Mr. Hart.

On the other hand, I felt like a dirty, little worm for
spying on him. "My instincts are as good as yours,
Daniel Fairhaven. I knew I was right."

"Right about what?" Bob Stanhope, Simon's
lawyer, was standing behind me. "Just what do you
think you're doing?"

Chapter Twelve

The Error of My Ways

"The civility which money will purchase is rarely extended to those who have none."

"Nothing."

I wasn't sure if I'd ever been so embarrassed. No doubt we both knew what I was doing rummaging through Simon's personal papers.

He lifted one—the bank statement—clearly the most damning. "Are you trying to decide how much Mr. Canterville is worth so you know how much to take him for? I take it he's not home. Do you have permission to go through his things?"

There were only so many ways I could play this. Fortunately being a writer also meant I was the world's best liar.

"You haven't heard? Mr. Canterville is in the hospital. They think someone tried to kill him right here in his own home."

"What?" He glanced around and then came back to me. "That's crazy. Who would want to kill Simon? And that still doesn't explain why I caught you going through his personal possessions."

"The hospital needs this information. He told me to come and get it for him." I smiled as sweet as honey. "I'm sure he'd love for you to visit him, Mr. Stanhope. They say he's going to be fine. But who knows for sure? I was just there this morning. He's so weak."

I also had a little actress in me and could summon crocodile tears pretty easily. Bob was uncomfortable with that and probably felt stupid that he hadn't known about Simon's attack.

"I'll take those papers to the hospital myself, Miss Wellman." He snatched them from me. "And don't think I won't check with Simon to be sure that he knew what you were doing."

For some reason I didn't understand, Bob didn't liked me. Maybe he just didn't know me well enough — or maybe he thought I was a gold digger like Ashcroft did. It was true that none of us really knew one another well.

I waited until Bob was gone and re-made copies of the papers Daniel needed. I went out to the garage to see if there was any way to dig my car out of the mass of boxes and furniture Simon and I had stored there. But my Beetle was as buried as the ancient Egyptian tombs. I might never see it again.

In the meantime, there was Simon's Bentley. It was old but well cared for. I was contemplating where he might keep the keys when Daniel pulled up in his car.

Steady, I advised myself. *Don't make eye contact. Stay a safe distance away. Don't make any promises.*

Fortified with my goals in mind, at least where Daniel was concerned, I went to meet him before he could knock on the door.

"There you are." His smile made my heart turn somersaults. "Did you find what I need?"

Careful. I stretched out my hand to give him the documents without touching him.

"Here they are. I didn't like doing it. I'm not doing it again." If my voice was unnecessarily rough, it was trying to hold back my emotions. I hoped he'd chalk it up to being upset about Simon.

"I understand. I'm sorry. I probably shouldn't have asked you. But thanks. Mr. Canterville will be grateful."

"Yeah. Whatever." I looked away from him with what I hoped was bored indifference. "I haven't seen any investigators out here. You didn't keep your side of the deal. Big surprise."

"Lisa, crime scene doesn't belong to me. I can't take them off other cases to look out here. But they'll be here. Okay?"

"I guess it has to be." *Don't look at him.*

"Okay. I'll take this back to the office and add it to the ever-growing pile of information that proves Mr. Canterville didn't kill Mr. Hart. I'll let you know if we get any new leads on who did."

"Fine. I'll be here."

"I wish you and I could talk. What about having some lunch? We could walk to that little bistro over there and watch the tourist boats go in and out. What do you say?"

No. No. No. Don't be stupid. You don't love him anymore. He doesn't love you. This is a pity lunch. Don't do it.

"Okay. Let me get my bag."

I slammed the door behind me as I went into the house. Was it too late to call him and tell him I couldn't go? He was waiting outside in the car. I didn't want to face him again. Maybe I could pretend to slip on one of the stairs and have a sprained ankle.

"No, I can't do that," I said to the empty house. "I can't write a protagonist who falls down all the time spraining her ankle. It's just wrong."

"Why are you talking to yourself?" Dickens asked as he appeared in front of me on the stairs. "Have you now lost your mind? Was it too much of a strain knowing that one of the world's greatest writers was offering to help you?"

He looked so smug and imperious. Seriously, why couldn't my ghost muse have been Agatha Christie?

"If you must know, it has absolutely nothing to do with you. I realize that's hard for you to imagine, since you have an ego the size of Mount Rushmore."

"How now? How do you know something like that about me?"

"You're all over the internet and in countless books. I think they even wrote a one-man play about you where someone pretends to be you." I could see his chest puffing out and his head going back to acknowledge the praises of him. "Great. Now you're even worse than before."

Maybe even being with Daniel was better than this. I ran up the stairs, hoping to get past him, but I still ended up going through part of him. It was like walking through a cold, damp cloud. I shivered but kept going.

He followed me. "What do you mean? I'd like to see all the available material about myself. No doubt most of it is incorrect. I would speak with the biographer who wrote this internet and the books about me. I assume he is a gentleman and a scholar."

I grabbed my handbag and thought about how worn my jeans and T-shirt were. I hadn't been planning to go out for lunch. I found a nicer top and clean jeans, running into the bathroom to change since Dickens was standing in the middle of my room.

Fussing with my hair in the mirror made me realize that I shouldn't have felt that way about Daniel. Not anymore. All these years I hadn't thought of him this way. I hadn't thought of him at all for days and weeks at a time.

Now here he was, back in my life because of Mr. Hart's death. I touched on some lipstick. And as soon as I saw him, I realized how much about him I remembered.

"If you're finished primping," Dickens said as I left the bathroom. "I want you to take me to this person. I believe we have a great deal to talk about."

"I'm going out for lunch. I'll be back soon. Try to get over yourself. There have been dozens of writers that were better than you—Twain, Hemmingway, Clancy. Maybe there are hundreds that were better than you. I'm leaving now. Try not to mess anything up while I'm gone."

I ran back down both flights of stairs as he yelled at me, calling me an impertinent wench and other much worse things. I locked the door as I ran out into the sunshine and saw Daniel leaning against his car, looking up at the place on the roof where Mr. Hart had been.

Slowing down before I looked too eager—as though running out wearing new clothes and lipstick wasn't bad enough—I finally stopped and looked up at the roof too.

"Are you seeing something different?" I asked, slightly out of breath from my headlong flight.

"Not exactly." He focused on me. "I was just thinking about all the ways someone could have put Mr. Hart on the roof."

"Good." I got in his car as he held the door open for me. "At least you're thinking in the right direction."

It wasn't far to the restaurant. We could've walked. But Daniel wanted to have the car close in case something came up. The day was bright and sunny, leaving the water blue and beautiful. Across the river was the red-brick naval hospital. Closer at hand were the tourist ferry boats that took passengers around the marina area and the visitor's bureau.

We were seated at a pretty table with a poinsettia in the middle. There was a generous amount of sparkling garland draped with lights across the walls and windows. Big-band Christmas tunes that I'd heard since I was a child like "Frosty the Snowman" played boldly, despite the fact that we were weeks before the holiday.

For the first time in twelve years, Daniel and I sat

across a table from each other alone. He ordered a cheeseburger and fries, like old times. I had a salad and a slice of pumpkin cheesecake. Like old times. I was always the sweet eater of the two of us.

Unlike old times, we were both edgy and uncertain about what to say. When we'd first met, it was all we could do to keep quiet for a few minutes. Now it was difficult.

Someone had to start somewhere, I decided. "Anything useful that you picked up from interviewing Ashcroft?"

He shook his head as he gulped ice water like he was on a desert planet. "I'm afraid not. With clear alibis for both events, we have to take him off the suspect list."

"Okay. There has to be someone. Who disliked Mr. Hart enough to kill him?"

"You mean besides you and Mr. Canterville?"

I met his eyes, sipped some soda, and looked away. "Obviously someone besides me and Simon. I realize that Simon's feud with Ebenezer was very public. But I'm sure there were other, less public disagreements that he had with people."

"He and his wife are involved in a messy divorce," he said. "She's asking for most of his financial portfolio and real estate."

"That sounds promising. I mean, in the way that we could find Mr. Hart's killer. What did he do for a living? I probably heard at some point, but I can't remember."

"He was an attorney, which was how he was able to make Mr. Canterville's life so difficult. He had an office in Olde Town in his basement, which surprised me since he was opposing any new business being set up there."

"That's always the way it is." I glanced at my watch and looked around for the waitress who'd taken our order.

"Are you in a hurry?" he asked.

"No. Not really. I'm expecting some people from a security service. I'm having an alarm system installed at the house."

The waitress brought our food and smiled at Daniel as she refilled his ice water. She wasn't as interested in me when she refilled my glass. Big surprise.

"Good idea. I guess you'll be able to open the book shop there with no issues. Does Canterville let you make those big financial decisions by yourself?"

"I asked him about this, as I always do." I sat forward a little and forgot my mantra about not looking him in the eyes. They were so blue. "Are you trying to say something about my relationship with Simon?"

"No, not at all. But Ashcroft made some valid points during his interview. I don't think it's surprising that he's suspicious of you. You're much younger than his father, and Canterville has pretty much given you carte blanche. I'd wonder about you too, if he was my father."

"I hope you set him right about me. I'm not after Simon's money."

He shrugged. "It's not my place to answer a suspect's questions. I know you. I know you're book crazy. This doesn't surprise me. I was just saying how I could imagine feeling if I was Ashcroft looking at your relationship with Simon from the outside."

"Book crazy? What does that even mean? And if it means what I think it means, what's wrong with it? It wouldn't hurt the world if there were more readers." I gestured wildly with my left hand and knocked his ice water in his lap.

Daniel immediately got to his feet with a shocked expression on his face. I grabbed the napkins on the table and started to blot the water from his suit when I realized where I was blotting and quickly stopped, my face burning.

"Oh, no!" Our waitress came quickly with a towel that she didn't seem to mind using on him, despite the sensitive area.

"Uh...thanks," he said, also red-faced. "I'll see if I can dry off in the men's room."

I figured that was the end of lunch and asked for what was left to be put in to-go bags while he was gone. It was probably just as well. He'd called me book crazy, for goodness sake. I wished I could have come up with some snarky retort right away, but as far as I knew, he had no passions besides his work. I could hardly call him crime crazy.

Besides, the moment had passed before I could come up with a suitable response. Why did that happen so often?

Daniel came out of the men's room with large, wet splotches on his pants. I hid my smile as he paid for lunch. Maybe I should have insisted on paying my part, but until the shop opened and I could share in the profits, I was on a limited budget.

We went back out to the car, and I peeked in the bags to make sure which one was his. He started the car without a word as I put his bag between us.

"I'm really sorry about the water. I hope you don't think I did it on purpose."

He looked at me. "Didn't you? If you didn't want to have lunch with me, all you had to do was say so."

"No. That wasn't it. I was gesturing after you said I was book crazy. It was an accident. I wouldn't do something so childish. I don't hate you."

"I don't hate you either."

"That's good then, right?"

"Right."

Chapter Thirteen

The Fall

"There is a wisdom of the head and a wisdom of the heart."

Why was this happening? Why now?

A thousand thoughts went through my mind. He smelled really nice. What would I do if he kissed me? Would his arms still feel as good around me?

Lucky for me, the sane thoughts outweighed the crazy ones pretty quickly.

"I'm going to walk home. I'll see you later." I grabbed my doggy bag as though my life depended on it and jumped out of the car.

Daniel got out too. "Wait a minute, Lisa. You don't have to walk home."

"I have to go home now. I'm sure you have things you should be doing too." I marched away. I was never getting in a car again with him. What had I been thinking?

He didn't follow me. I was glad. At least the smart, logical part of my brain was glad. There was a reason we'd gotten divorced. It had nothing to do with kissing or any other biological aspect of our relationship. It had to do with us being two very different people who couldn't live together.

The way my heart was still pounding as I crossed the street, I knew I needed to go home and write that a million times like teachers made students do in school. Instead of *I shall not talk in class*, I needed to write *I shall not forget why Daniel Fairhaven and I can't be together.*

My anger and fear got me all the way back to Simon's house. I could tell no one from the crime scene unit had been there yet. It was something I could put all my anger and frustration into. I put my handbag and doggy bag on the porch by the front door and went to the garage to take out the ladder.

It would probably have been easier to climb out on the roof from my bedroom window, but I didn't want to have to go through dozens of questions from the ghost. I put the ladder up against the house and got an envelope from my bag to add any evidence I found from the roof.

Anger and fear propelled me up the lowest end of the roof and started me climbing across the shingles toward the window in the turret. The wind whipped across my hair, blowing strongly from the river, making me regret the anger and fear that was rapidly leaving me. I paused to look at the wonderful view of the water and the other rooftops that surrounded the house. I was surprised to see how many roofs had Christmas decorations on them. I hadn't noticed them from the ground.

I had reached the spot, outlined in chalk or paint, where Ebenezer Hart's body had been. I sat and studied it, wishing I'd also brought a pen or pencil to make a drawing of the spot. Of course I didn't need to do that since my phone was in my pocket and I could take a picture. Many mystery writers hated having cell phones in their books, feeling that it made the plot too easy to solve. I never felt that way. A writer had to work around cell phones sometimes by utilizing their weaknesses—dropped calls, no signal, dead batteries. But it enhanced modern mysteries.

After taking several pictures of the spot where the body had been from different angles, the wind blew a strong gust my way, and I dropped my phone. It rattled across the roof before falling into the bushes down below.

"That's fine," I told myself with a careful look over the edge. "At least I got the pictures."

"What in God's name are you doing out here?" Dickens popped his head through the shingles, startling me, and I lost my balance, following the path of my cell phone off the edge and toward the ground.

"It's fine. It's fine," I babbled, knowing it wasn't fine. A cell phone could fall into the bushes, and nothing would happen to it. A person probably couldn't do the same. In fact, I knew I couldn't because I'd gone to ten seminars about what happened to people who fell from heights. How far up was I anyway — thirty feet?

It was amazing how many things went through my head as I fell. It was like time slowed down to give me the opportunity to consider everything. It was exactly as people described the moments before their deaths where their whole lives flashed before them.

I saw my mother when I was young and immediately before she died. I saw Daniel and me together, happy, as we graduated from college. I saw my first cat, Pinky, and the car that ran over her. The driver had offered me a chocolate bar if I didn't tell my parents.

"And I don't have anything to write it down," I yelled, though I doubted I would ever forget what I'd seen as I fell. If I survived, I'd have a whole new perspective on killing my characters by pushing them off houses and other places. For that matter, I'd have a great new idea about my protagonist falling too. It was going to be amazing.

If I survive.

Suddenly time sped up, and I fell faster. My arms flailed the empty space around me, but there was nothing to hold on to. What a stupid way to die. I hoped they'd spell my name correctly in the obituary and add in something about my budding career as a mystery writer.

Then there was a dull thud.

It didn't hurt. I thought I'd hit the ground, but that wasn't it. I could still see the ground around me. This was something else — like someone caught me as I fell. But that wasn't possible from that height, especially since my weight didn't seem to affect the person who'd managed it. Research told me that such a person would have to fall to the ground under my weight. Firefighters did it and were injured but saved a life. It was possible.

But unlikely.

I looked into the strange face that was near mine. She seemed to be an older lady, completely dressed in black and wearing a black hood. Her eyes were a rare shade of green surrounded by thousands of fine wrinkles.

What in the world?

"Who are you? How did you catch me? Are you okay?"

The woman set me on my feet like I was a toy. "I am Aine of Ulster. My companion and I are searching for Daniel Fairhaven. Have you seen him?"

It was impossible to describe her voice—like sandpaper and glass shards to the ear. I wanted to use the word *unearthly*—and I would when I wrote about her. This was too good not to put in a book.

She was tall and obviously strong, since she'd managed to catch me. I'm no lightweight with my love for all things sweet when I was nervous or excited. I glanced up at the roof and then back at her. "That was remarkable. How is it even possible?"

"You were falling after the ghost scared you on the roof. I caught you." She shrugged as thought it was nothing.

"Ghost? You saw Dickens?"

"Excuse me." A man's voice hailed me from behind. "I'm Detective Sean O'Neill of the Norfolk Police Department."

I turned to him. He was a normal, average, good-looking guy in a decent suit. He showed me his badge, not that I doubted him. I was just too amazed to have survived the fall and been caught in the arms of an Amazon woman to return his greeting. I wanted to hug and kiss the woman who'd saved me, but there was something distinctly foreboding about her.

"I'm so sorry." I laughed to cover all the jumbled emotions running through me. My heart was still pounding. I would never forget that feeling of falling. "I'm Lisa Wellman. I'm friends with Daniel, but he's not here right now."

"Where has he gone? We can use his blood to track him. Have you some?" Aine said without a trace of a smile on her face. She was serious.

"She's kidding." Detective O'Neill glared at her and then smiled at me. "Have you seen him today? I understood he was out here working on a case. He's my liaison to the Portsmouth police. We're helping out with a murder that was involved with a drug sting."

"Yes, I just had lunch with him. I can call him for you. Would you like to come up on the porch to wait?"

"That would be nice. This is a wonderful old house. Is this the place I read about online that you're trying to open as a book shop?"

"It is." I led the way to the porch. "We've had some issues, but I think they're sorting themselves out now. Would you like some tea?"

"No, thanks." Detective O'Neill sat in one of the white, wicker chairs. "I guess that's good news for you."

"All but the murder that occurred here." Aine was still standing. She sniffed the air around us. "Is it the ghost of the man who was killed?"

"No. He's been here since yesterday, but he's not the man who was killed. He says he's Charles Dickens, the writer, from England. I have no idea how he got here or what he's really doing here. He keeps saying he's here to help my writing. Mostly he's just been a big pain."

"I would be honored to exorcise him." She lowered her head to me in almost a full bow.

"You're Irish, aren't you?" I suddenly noticed the accent. Well, I did just fall off the roof.

"I am indeed. I was once Queen of Ulster, but that was many years before my death. I have since served the O'Neill family. It would be my pleasure to rid you of the annoying parasite."

"Aine doesn't have firm grip on the American language yet." Detective O'Neill was glaring at her again. "She's my assistant, and she knows nothing about ghosts except what she's seen on TV."

"That is not true, O'Neill," Aine argued. "Ghosts can be annoying, even preying on the living."

They had a staring match that lasted long enough until Daniel arrived. I hadn't even had a chance to call him.

"Sean." Daniel got out of the car, calling his name. "I just got your message. Sorry I was late. You didn't have to drive over here. I was on my way back to the office."

I refused to indulge my desire to look at him. "It was nice meeting you, Detective O'Neill. You too, Aine. Thank you again for saving my life. I have some work to do."

It was rude. My mother would've been the first to point it out. But my recent emotional outburst with

Daniel had left me feeling raw. I let myself into the house, watching out the window as Detective O'Neill introduced Aine to Daniel. They all shook hands and went to their cars that were parked at the curb.

I sat in a chair near the sofa and cuddled with Truffles. Maggie May jumped up on my lap and started cleaning herself. Wordsworth tried to jump on the chair, but his short legs wouldn't get him up that high. Puck was in a corner staring at us as though he thought we were crazy. He just wasn't the cuddling type, still a little wild after his time on the street. Maybe later.

"My deepest sympathies, madam." Dickens nodded to me. "It was not my intention to frighten you from the roof. I am happy to see that you are uninjured."

"Thanks." I took a deep breath and looked around at all the work that still needed to be done in time for our Thanksgiving weekend opening. I had to admit that it seemed more real with Mr. Hart out of the picture. I hoped Simon would be well enough for it.

There was a knock at the door. Two crime scene techs introduced themselves and showed me their badges. They were there to check on the roof and the ground around the outside of the house as well as Simon's bedroom. They'd be dusting for prints there and looking for whatever else they could find that might tell us who'd poisoned Simon.

As they were getting started, the security company showed up. That included two installers and a salesman who tried to convince me to buy the upgrade package. Without knowing how much money the book shop would bring in, I had to disappoint him. I didn't want Simon to be deeply in debt to follow his dream.

While everyone did what they were there to do, I went outside and searched for my cell phone. It was in the bushes where I'd thought it would be. The greenery had broken its fall. Not even the screen was cracked. The phone and I were both fortunate.

I spent the next few hours ignoring everyone and taking books out of boxes. It was a difficult task because I had the urge to stop and look at each one. There were first-run copies of *Tom Sawyer* and of *Huckleberry Finn*. I found a beautifully illustrated edition of *Peter Pan* that I caught myself thumbing through with a reader's thrill of finding a treasure. There were also older copies of *Gone with the Wind* and *To Kill a Mockingbird*.

The books were categorized and put in their appropriate rooms. There were large books and tiny books of romantic poetry. I tried to keep their sizes together to make for easier browsing. We'd need signs that indicated the oversized books and the smaller ones too.

I enjoyed looking at the wonderful graphics of the older work and reading parts of my favorites from Ray Bradbury and Andre Norton. The mystery room was filling up quickly with Agatha Christie, Raymond Chandler, and many others. I was trying to decide if I should put the gothics from authors like Mary Stewart into another room when I noticed it was almost four-thirty.

Wanting to have dinner at the hospital with Simon to fill him in on everything that had happened, I checked around the house to make sure the security team and the crime scene units were gone. Both of them had opened the front door to yell out that they were leaving. I hadn't paid much attention since I was engrossed in my book world.

But they were gone. I set the alarm the way the salesman had shown me to be a perimeter alert and went upstairs to take a shower. Dickens was poring over the papers on my desk. He looked up as I came in.

"This is really not as bad as I'd thought," he said. "It needs work, no doubt. And a good polish. Your grammar and spelling are atrocious. But that can be said for most writers. I myself never had that problem, but I was unusual."

"Thanks. Do you mind going somewhere else? I need a quick shower and a change of clothes. We can talk about this later." *Unless I get lucky, and Dana can figure out something to do about you.*

"I saw you looking through the books and shelving them. I believe dedicating a room to my work would not be out of order. Ebenezer Scrooge and Tim Cratchit are some of the most popular characters in the world."

"I wouldn't say popular. Maybe well-loved. Your books are read in schools quite a bit now, but most people know Scrooge and Marley from movies and plays." I didn't feel too bad letting him down. He didn't seem to mind criticizing my work.

"That is absurd! I shall take a look at the other books you plan to stock here at your shop. Perhaps you might want to reconsider having more of my books than you planned."

He disappeared, and I was glad to see him go. It had been a long, exhausting day already. I still wanted to go to the hospital and meet back here with Dana later.

The shower felt good, energizing me for the rest of

the day. I hummed as I dressed up my hair with a green scarf and added some lipstick. The scarf matched a skirt and sweater set that I'd worn at the library many times. I thought seeing me in it might be comforting for Simon after all he'd been through.

There was no sign of Dickens. *Whew!* I really didn't need him around right now. How could he have ended up here anyway? I had to remind myself that he might not really be a ghost. I couldn't wait to talk to Dana about it.

I looked pretty good when I grabbed my bag and started out the front door, hoping not to attract attention from Dickens before I could go. I set the alarm for inside and outside, quickly closing the door behind me.

"Lisa."

Daniel was about to knock on the door, and I caught my breath, getting tired of surprises that day.

"Yes. What is it?" My tone mirrored my impatience.

"You look wonderful." His eyes went slowly from my head to my green heels, lingering in a few spots that made me nervous. "Hot date?"

"I'm eating dinner with Simon. What do you want?"

"I thought you might like to hear what the crime scene team found in and around the house. If you're busy, I can come back later."

The door was closed and locked. The alarm was set. But I was interested in what he had to say. I invited him to sit on the porch and tell me everything.

"Maybe I should just go with you to talk to Simon. He should hear this firsthand, since it is his house and

everything."
  Oh, no.

Chapter Fourteen

The Truth and Nothing But the Truth

"Oh the nerves, the mystery of this machine called man."

"That's not a good idea. Simon is still recovering. He might react better hearing the information from me."

It was as good an excuse as I could come up with not to spend time with him going to the hospital.

"It's not just a matter of him hearing this," he assured me. "I need to ask him a few questions about the information. He might feel better if you're there too."

How could I argue with that?

"That's fine." I drew in a deep, exasperated breath. "But I'll drive."

"Great." He eyed the Bentley in the drive. "I've always wanted to ride in one of those. It's in great shape too."

"What? No. That's not what I meant. You drive your car, and I'll drive mine." I smiled to make the words less harsh. "You always say you don't want to be far from your car in case duty calls, right?"

He looked away and ran his hand through his red hair as the afternoon breeze teased it. "Look, I didn't mean to make you nervous this afternoon. I'm sorry. Sometimes I forget that we've been apart for so long."

So he'd felt it too? All the more reason not to get in any car with him.

"It wasn't your fault. You don't have to apologize." *And I don't want to talk about it.* "If you're coming with me, let's go. I have a meeting tonight."

"Book Shop Owners of America?" he quipped.

"No. Paranormal investigators." I opened the driver's side door.

"Writing a mystery with ghosts in it?" He walked around the back of the car to the passenger side.

"Yes. Maybe. She's a friend of mine from a writing group."

"Uh oh." He stopped at the back of the Bentley. "Your tag is expired. I guess we'll be taking my car after all."

I stormed to the back and glanced at the plate. "It's only a month past due. Surely there must be some leeway."

"Did you give people leeway when they brought in

an overdue library book?" He watched my face. "That's what I thought. Let's take my car."

As soon as he had walked away, I kicked the Bentley's bumper in frustration. This just wasn't my day.

I had a little talk with myself on the way to his car. It wasn't a big deal. Nothing crazy was going to happen between us. There was nothing to worry about.

After that personal conversation, I sauntered over to his car where he stood holding the door open and got inside. My skirt got caught when he closed the door, but I corrected it right away.

Eyes facing forward. No more intimate conversations or bringing up things that had happened in the past. I pretended that Daniel was a taxi driver with something in the back seat so I couldn't ride there. He started the car, and we drove away.

"I heard what happened to you on the roof," he said. "Well, off the roof. That was amazing that Aine Ulster could catch you without breaking something."

Biting my tongue on an immediate retort, I nodded. "Yes. But her name was Aine *of* Ulster. She never mentioned a last name."

"O'Neill didn't make a move without her. I was wondering if she ever let him out of her sight. She's a good partner."

"Yes, she is." *Wood. I'm made of wood. Nothing you say can bother me.*

"I guess you weren't hurt anyway, huh?" He glanced at me. "What were you doing up there?"

"I was looking for fiber remnants to prove someone could have hauled Mr. Hart up there with a rope."

"You knew someone was coming out to look at

that. You could've waited."

"I thought it might rain before they got there. Fall is the rainy season."

"Well, the crime scene techs didn't find any remnants of rope. There weren't any noticeable shoe prints either. I'm afraid we're still stuck with the idea that the dead man was pushed out of your window."

"I think I just proved that the pitch on the roof over there would have made him fall to the ground just as I did. Unless he was dead already, and just stayed there."

"But we're back to how he got up there. I can't think of any other way the killer could have gotten him in that position."

"Someone could have carried him up there. The ladder was outside. I used it to get up there. Anyone else could have done the same." I warned myself that I was losing control of the conversation. There shouldn't have been a conversation. What was I doing? I couldn't let him goad me into an argument.

"Mr. Hart weighted almost two hundred pounds. It would take a strong man to get him up there on a ladder." Daniel glanced at me when we stopped at the light.

I could see the hospital right in front of us. It would only take a few more minutes to pull in there and park. We'd be inside and going to Simon's room quickly. All I had to do was keep my wits about me. Wouldn't that be what I expected from a protagonist in my book?

"Or a fireman." I couldn't help myself. It was like the words wouldn't stop coming out of my mouth. "A fireman has to be able to carry at least a hundred and sixty pounds. A stronger fireman could carry more."

Daniel pulled the car into the parking deck. He was allowed to park in a special area for police cars. I made a note of that as I quickly got out of the car.

He came around to my side and gazed fiercely into my eyes. "You just want to argue with me, don't you? You don't really think you know more about investigating crime than I do because you're a mystery writer. That would be crazy."

I pushed the up button on the elevator. *Come on. Come on.* "I guess that would go along with me being a crazy book lady."

"Is everything I say to you wrong?"

The elevator finally got there. Two older ladies got out with smiles and nods for us. We got in the empty elevator with terrible music playing. I was prepared not to answer his question. Only two floors and we'd be at Simon's wing. His room was close to the elevator. It was going to be okay.

"Not everything, I suppose." The wicked voice inside me answered him as some other terrible part of me made me turn my head to face him. "There were times when everything was right between us."

Where had that come from? I didn't even think it was my voice. It had to be some demon that had crept inside me. I would never have provoked him that way.

"Lisa," he whispered as he stepped toward me, his eyes alight with passion.

I had already closed my eyes for his kiss. But the elevator was smarter than me. It chimed as the doors opened on the second floor. My heart pounded. I could barely think. I stumbled out the door and made it to the white tile floor. Somehow I'd been saved at the last minute despite my own foolish actions.

"Here we are. I'll race you to Simon's room."

Naturally there was no sprint down the short hall between the elevator and Simon's room—just me and Daniel glaring at each other. We couldn't be together without either wanting to kiss or kill one another. And after all this time—it was crazy.

Simon was awake and alert when we reached him. "Good to see you both. Gets lonely here, even with those confounded Florence Nightingales asking me every five minutes how I feel. I feel like going home. Tell me you come bearing good news."

Daniel let me tell Simon everything that had happened. I'd taken a seat by the bed, but Daniel stood there like some large bird of prey, eyes narrowed, ready to pounce if he thought Simon was lying or giving himself away as Mr. Hart's killer.

"So you got the alarm system in." Simon sniffed. "I suppose I shall need to have the code tattooed on my wrist so I can remember it. Bloody nuisance, that. But a sign of the times, I suppose. I remember when people never even locked their doors and you could leave your bike on the green with no cause for worry."

"In the meantime, Mr. Canterville, I had some techs go over your house. I don't have that information back yet. I hope we'll get some idea about who tried to poison you. Now that you're in a better state of mind, can you shed any light on that?"

"No, Detective. I wish I could. Makes a man feel helpless to be poisoned in his own home. I can't remember a thing of what happened."

"What about the murder of Ebenezer Hart? Is there anything you can add to what we already have that could solve this case?"

Simon thought a moment. "I truly have no idea why anyone would want to kill Hart and leave him on my roof. Bad show and all, you know."

"So far you had the strongest motive to kill Mr. Hart," Daniel continued. "He was trying to stop your book shop from opening. That alone might cause someone to consider killing him." He glanced at me. "You and Lisa are both on top of the list of suspects."

"There are so many things wrong with that concept, young man." Simon's blue eyes were fierce. "Perhaps you should look to your own skills as a detective. Widen your search, sir."

Daniel nodded without arguing as his phone rang, and he took the call out of the room.

"Never mind him," I said, smiling. "How are you feeling? I hope you're still ready to go home tomorrow."

"I'm ready to go now, my dear Miss Wellman." He nodded toward the door. "I believe that young man has emotional problems. I've met others like him. Difficult for them to get past their own issues, you know." He chortled. "Of course when a man's heart is involved, his business suffers. Dickens said that. A brilliant man, and one of the few to earn true recognition during his lifetime."

"Dickens?" A shiver went through me. "It's funny you should mention that because—"

"It looks like we have a new lead on Mr. Hart's killer." Daniel burst into the room, full of energy. "I have to go, Lisa. Can you catch a taxi home?"

"Not a problem." *In fact, I'd run all the way home rather than get in the car with you again.*

"Thanks." He nodded to Simon. "Mr. Canterville. I

hope you're up and about soon, sir."

"Appreciate it, Detective. Good luck catching Hart's killer."

Simon's dinner came right after Daniel left. I went down to the cafeteria for a sandwich. We talked about the book shop and the progress I'd made getting the books out of the boxes while we ate.

"After I get out of this accursed place, we'll get at it like barnstormers. Never fear. Canterville's book shop will be open by Thanksgiving."

We toasted with his glass of ginger ale and my bottle of water. I didn't tell him that he would still have to rest for a few days after his experience. We could always discuss that when he was finally home again.

"I feel that we should change the name of the shop," he said. "I could not do this without you. I believe the name should be Canterville and Wellman. It seems more fitting to me."

"Maybe we could talk about that later," I suggested. "We've spent thousands of dollars on signs, banners, business cards, and advertisement. There wouldn't be time to change everything and still be open by the deadline."

"I apologize for not thinking of it sooner. You must allow that an old man can be too caught up in what's going on until he finds himself flat on his back in a place like this. As soon as there is time to make that change, Miss Wellman, I think that's exactly what we should do."

"Thank you for thinking of it, Simon." I put my hand on his. "I really like Canterville's Book Shop better anyway. But let's see." Glancing at my watch, I got to my feet. "I have to go. I'll call first thing tomorrow to find out if and when you're being released. Have a good night."

"You're a pip. Thank you for all that you do. I'll see you tomorrow."

It wasn't hard to imagine why Simon and Ashcroft didn't get along. I was close enough to Simon to think it was all Ashcroft's fault, but my writer's brain made me realize that there could be many reasons why a father and son didn't like each other. One thing about being a writer was that you had to be impartial and able to see more than one character's point of view in a story.

Because I was still low on funds, I didn't call a taxi. I could have taken the bus, but I decided to walk. There was a chill in the air, but the streets were full of lights and sounds. It was good to be out with the world and observing everything to be able to call on the information later. Even the man walking a trio of tiny dogs in Santa hats was fodder for some spot in a future book.

It wasn't more than a few minutes before I started thinking about my protagonist who was locked in the large, dark house with a monster storm bearing down on her and nowhere to hide.

There was more going on inside the old manor on the Atlantic coast—obviously, since she'd lost her memory somehow. It wasn't important for me to know right now what had caused her memory loss. Being a 'pantser,' I was ready to let that story, and my own, unfold.

Chapter Fifteen

In the Lurch

"He would make a lovely corpse."

Dana Schwartz arrived at the house exactly at seven p.m. She'd brought her entire crew with her to check out the house. That included a computer person, a photographer, and a psychic. I was surprised by the psychic since I knew Dana was purely into the science of ghosts.

"I bring Becky in to contact the spirit. It sounds crazy, but there do seem to be some people who are more in tune with the spirit world and can call them out."

We walked through the entire house from basement to third floor. Dana made notes with her phone recorder while Becky walked around, getting a 'vibe' on the house. Darren set up his computer, and Tommy got his multi-spectrum cameras and video equipment ready.

"The funny thing is," I told her, "I haven't seen Dickens around since I got home from the hospital. Maybe he left. I was kind of hard on him for scaring me off the roof."

She laughed, her short, bouncy, blond hair bobbing around her pretty face. Her eyes were large and blue. She always wore blue or purple to emphasize them.

"That's the way it always is. Don't forget, if there's a ghost here, he can hear you. He knew you were planning to bring us in. It doesn't surprise me that he'd leave when he knew what you're doing."

I guessed that made sense. "Have you ever actually seen a real ghost—besides that one you told me about when you were a kid?"

The skeptic in me tended to be wary of ghost stories from Dana's eight-year-old self. Her father had died then, and she'd seen him dozens of times. It was what had gotten her started in ghost hunting.

"Better than that," she said. "Tommy has pictures of some of them. Wait 'til we get back downstairs, and I'll show you. All four of us have seen really scary stuff, Lisa. Sometimes there ends up being a rational explanation for it. Other times, it's just a ghost."

"How's your book about ghost hunting coming along?" I asked as we went downstairs.

"Good." She grinned. "Not agent/editor good, but it's coming along. How are you doing on your WIP?"

That's WIP—work in progress. Someday, I promised myself, I was going to write a whole book about writing acronyms. "It's slow, but with moving and helping get the book shop set up, it's not surprising."

"Not to mention giving up your job at the library after so many years, your mother's death, and all the trauma that went with that." She put her arm around me and squeezed tight for a moment. "Cut yourself some slack. You deserve a breather. Looks like this is gonna be a sweet deal for you once everything is up and running. I love your room."

It made me feel a lot better for her to say that. I didn't have any choice about selling my mother's house to pay her medical bills, but I could've stayed with Liz or found an apartment. I was sure that's what Daniel was thinking—*why is she living in this old house with one room to call her own?*

"I knew you'd understand," I told her. "It's hard to work a full-time job and get any writing done. This way, if things are slow, I can pop up to my bedroom and work for a while. I'm hoping to have my book done by next year at this time. We'll see."

"Where have you seen the ghost in the house?" Becky asked as she drifted by us on the stairs. "I'm getting strong vibes everywhere. He's manifested all over the house, hasn't he?"

"Yes. Is that a bad thing?"

"Not bad. Unusual. Spirits are mostly contained to a single room or area. Have you seen him outside?"

"He poked his head out of the roof when I was up there," I told her. "I'm just wondering why Charles Dickens would be here at all."

Becky shrugged. She was short and extremely thin, completely dressed in black.

"Maybe it's all these old books," she suggested. "Maybe he's drawn to them."

"Maybe," I half agreed. "But if he was drawn to old books, wouldn't he want to be back in his hometown or at least somewhere in his own country?"

"It could be anything," she continued. "Maybe he feels a kinship to you, since you're both writers. Maybe he just likes the vibes here. They're really strong. This place might be built on an old cemetery or a ley line."

I couldn't speak to that since it wasn't my house. I wasn't even sure if Simon had lived here more than a few years. The house might not even be from his family.

"I'm going to wander around a bit more to get a feel for the place," Becky said. "I'll meet you downstairs when I'm ready to start."

Dana took me to the computer area where Darren was setting up. She asked him to show me some pictures from their last few ghost-hunting sessions. One group of pictures was taken on the Cooper River Bridge in Charleston, South Carolina. Another group was from the Naval Hospital.

"How did you get them to let you take your equipment in there?" I asked, looking at the scary pictures of white figures and other images the cameras had captured.

"We were visiting my grandpa," Dana admitted. "Might as well take a few shots while we were there, right? The hospital is seven points on the scare meter. I can't tell you how many stories I've heard from people who have worked there or been there for medical reasons. Even my own mother had a few tales to tell from when I was born."

"These images are so amazing. How could anyone see them and not believe there are ghosts in the world?"

She smiled. "Actually, I'm reserving judgement on that. I find that people who are creative — like you — are more likely to believe. People who don't have creative energy and thought processes are harder to convince. How long did it take for you to accept that the ghost of Charles Dickens was standing in front of you?"

I thought back to him trying to scare me. "I guess not that long. He did a fair imitation of the scene from *A Christmas Carol* when Marley first visits Scrooge. That convinced me."

"That's exciting."

"Maybe that's because Dickens was creative too," Darren said. "Maybe creative types make more interesting ghosts. Let's see if we can set up at the library, Dana."

"I'm ready." Becky came slowly down the stairs to the ground floor.

"Okay." Dana nodded at her. "Lisa, it might be best if you stay out of the way. Take a seat right over there and let us do our stuff."

I sat in one of the chairs with an embroidered seat and waited to see what would happen. The computer was ready. All the cameras were in place. Becky put her hands to her temples and closed her eyes before she called for Dickens to come forward.

Nothing happened. We waited two hours and still no sign of Dickens. I was a little embarrassed. Not that I had any control over when and where he appeared. For all I knew, he was tired of me and had moved on, since I wasn't working as hard on my book as he thought I should. Or maybe I had imagined the whole thing. I might not have seen him at all—although what a weird character for me to have chosen as a ghost to haunt me.

"I think we should change rooms, even though he's been all over the house." Dana called it. "Where has he been seen most frequently?"

"Maybe more important," Becky contradicted her. "Where did he manifest outside?"

"Well, he first came to me in the turret room where I sleep. And he stuck his head out of the roof." I thought about what I was saying. Did I want everyone up in my room looking for the ghost of Christmas past?

Too late.

"I'll leave the computer down here," Darren said. "I can take the tablet up with me and still stay connected."

"I'll move a few of the cameras," Tommy said.

"Maybe going up there will make a difference," Dana explained as she picked up her notebooks and started upstairs. Becky followed. They left me as they moved to my bedroom.

"Your friends are quite unusual," Dickens said when they were gone. "They search for ghosts, do they?"

"They're here to help me understand if I'm insane and you don't exist at all or if you're real why you'd choose to come here." Of course he was probably there the whole time and just refusing to show himself.

"Gad! Why didn't you say so? I can explain much better, being of this realm we call spirit. Of course you haven't lost your mind, Lisa. I would never spend time with someone insane. Just one moment and we shall have further discourse on the subject." He smiled in a way that made his face transform into something more frightening.

"No. Wait."

Unfortunately spirits don't need stairs or legs. As I was sprinting up the iron, spiral staircase, Dana and the others screamed. They ran out of my room and down the stairs. Becky almost knocked me down trying to escape.

"What's going on?" I asked, though no one paused to explain. I had no choice but to go up to my room in order to get away from their downward flight. My room was a wreck, things strewn everywhere. It was going to be a pain to put right again. I shook my head, knowing I should have been more careful with what I said.

Turning around and going right back down because I was afraid my work on the books would all be undone, I found Tommy, Dana, and Darren on the ground floor laughing. Had they lost their minds?

"What's wrong with you?" I asked, noticing that the front door was open and the psychic gone. "Where's Becky?"

"She took off," Dana said between bouts of laughter.

"Nothing's wrong," Darren hooted, high fiving Tommy. "Nothing could be better. I wish I had a magnum of champagne to celebrate."

"That's right," Tommy agreed. "This is the motherlode. It's what every ghost chaser hopes to find. We actually saw a floating, full-figure apparition that spoke to us. It doesn't get better than this."

Well, I'd told Dickens what I needed, and he supplied it. I wasn't crazy unless they were too—which at the moment seemed possible. But he'd appeared in front of them.

"Did you get pictures?"

"Unbelievable images!" Darren sat at his computer and pulled them up so we could look at them. There was Dickens in ghost form. He levitated things around my bedroom and spouted quotes from his work. He did everything he could to prove to me and them that he was real.

"Wait until word gets out about this," Dana predicted. "This place will be listed on the *Most Haunted* website. People will come here from all over the world to see this. Scientists will want to set up and study this house."

Suddenly what Dickens had done didn't sound as good. "I don't think that would work for a book shop," I told her.

"Someone will buy this place from you, Lisa, and it will become a hotbed of paranormal studies. Who needs a book shop when you could have something like that?"

This definitely wasn't good or what I'd had in mind.

"Dana, you can't tell everyone. I want this place to be a book shop. Someday, I hope to have a signing here for my first book. You could have your first book signing here too. But not if it's been taken over by people looking for ghosts."

I could see the warring factions in her face. Amazing paranormal opportunity. Or book shop where new writers were welcome.

"I guess you're right, Lisa." She shrugged. "I got carried away by this experience. Do you know how rare this is? I don't know why the ghost of Charles Dickens is here, but I'm so glad I got to see him. Thank you." She gazed up at the ceiling. "Thank you too, Mr. Dickens. I loved *A Christmas Carol*."

Darren was surprised by her decision to not go public with what had happened. "This stuff is too good not to share with the paranormal community. We could be the grand prize winners at the next Ghost Hunters Expo. We can't just turn our backs on this."

"I agree with Darren," Tommy said. "I may never take pictures again like these. These are prize-winning pics. We can't ignore that."

"You heard what the lady said," Dana replied. "If this gets out, she loses the book shop. I don't want that on my conscience, do you?"

Tommy looked at Darren. "I could live with that."

"Yeah," Darren agreed. "Me too."

"Well, I'm sorry," Dana said. "But I can't. We can't release these photos or videos. Got it?"

Both men nodded and began packing up.

"Thanks," I said to her. "I'm sorry. I guess I really didn't think you'd see anything since I wasn't even sure it was real."

"Don't fret over it," she replied with a smile. "I'm just really glad I was here for it. Thank you, Lisa. I'll see you tomorrow night for the writer's meeting."

I watched them leave with mixed emotions. They'd verified what was going on, but it left me uneasy.

"Do you think they will keep their mouths shut?" Dickens asked.

"I don't know. You did such a good job of

convincing them, it's impossible to say."

Chapter Sixteen

Spirited Help

"Procrastination is the thief of time, collar him."

"How shall I ever understand this world?"

Dickens had been quoting himself for the last hour while I'd tried to work on my manuscript. It was difficult to shut him out, but I'd persevered to get several pages written.

"What is this device you are working on?" He finally stopped ranting and stood beside me. "And what is this that you're writing? If this woman was any more pathetic, she would not be alive. You need to revise your story."

"Revise it? I've barely written enough on it to have the beginning of a story."

"And the lighted device?"

"It's called a computer. You type on it like a typewriter, and the words are stored inside."

"Remarkable."

I turned to face him. "Why are you here? And don't tell me that you're here to help me solve Mr. Hart's death or write my book. Why are you really here?"

He paced the floor though his feet didn't touch it. "I am here to ask for your help, Miss Wellman. It may not be important to you, but there was one novel that I did not see through to its end."

"*The Mystery of Edwin Drood.* I know. I've read all about it. You had a stroke before you could finish. What does that have to do with me?"

"I wish I could tell you. Something about your work called to me—even to the very grave where I lie. I cannot help but feel there is a kindred between us. You remind me something of myself, though I see little of my ambition in you."

"What are you trying to say?"

"I should like your help completing my novel." He puffed out his chest and held up his head so that his beard nearly stuck straight out from his face. "I realize it is a singular honor to be asked by an author of my stature to aid me in finishing. Yet still I ask it."

My mouth had dropped open at his request. Put aside my work to help a dead man with a project no one would ever see because no one would believe it?

"You know people have finished the book for you. In fact, they even wrote a musical about it."

"What?" he thundered, his anger shaking the room.

"Why is it that this time makes musical theater out of my work? How am I to respond to such a thing? What I find most amazing is that there would be something entertaining about an opium addict and a murder. What is wrong with you people?"

"I don't know why people make musicals out of your work. But you died without finishing the story, and people wanted an ending, even if they had to write one themselves. Would you like to see it? I believe they had Jasper kill Edwin and put him in the church crypt. Or was he murdered by his rival, Neville Landless? I'm not sure. It was a while ago that I read it."

"This is preposterous!" he continued raging. "What right had they to finish what I began? Could they not wait for me to find a way to complete my work?"

"It's been, like, a hundred and fifty years since you died," I said. "I don't think anyone expected you to come back and finish the story."

I thought he might explode, but instead he nudged me sharply out of the chair and put himself at my desk in front of my computer.

"Teach me. I have always been a quick study. Teach me to use this device to actually complete my work."

From the floor where he'd pushed me, I said, "That won't work. You're a ghost. I don't think you can type."

He studied the keyboard and monitor. "I am certain I can use this contraption. How does it work?"

"It's not that much different than the old typewriters, which I think were around when you were alive. You spell words by tapping your fingers on the keys." I showed him.

"Yes. I'm aware of the typing machines." He impatiently struck his fingers against the keyboard. The monitor went black with a fizzling sound in the wiring. "Confound it, madam. This infernal thing won't work."

"All right. Let's think about this. I'll see if I can get the computer running again, and I'll type while you dictate." I thought it was the least I could do for a fellow writer. It was a nuisance, but how would I feel if I'd died during a book?

The sun was rising, making prisms on the windows in my room, and the sky was already blue, shining on the river. The day was about to begin. There wasn't time to get this going before I had to take a shower, get dressed, pick up Simon—I hoped—and get going on putting the books where they belonged.

"Let's get back to this tonight," I said. "If I can get the computer fixed by then, okay?"

"I suppose it shall have to be so." He harrumphed. His skinny beard disappeared into the folds of his white shirt. "But I shall hold you to it. I know you slack at your own work. You shall not slack at mine. My time here is limited."

He curtly nodded and disappeared.

Letting out a sigh of relief, I fell back on the bed, exhausted. I knew helping him was the right thing. I just hoped I could keep up with everything that was expected of me in the next few weeks.

I didn't realize that I'd fallen asleep until I heard pounding at the front door. It barely penetrated my consciousness and I yawned before I got up and headed downstairs.

It was Daniel. He looked fit to be tied, as my mother used to say. He threw down a newspaper on the table in the foyer. "What's up with this? You could've done this any other time, Lisa. In the middle of a homicide investigation wasn't one of them."

Only half awake, I glanced at the paper. The headline made my eyes bug open quickly: "Controversial Book Shop in Olde Town Now Sets Sights on Spirits."

"What? She promised they wouldn't say anything. Simon is going to kill me. How are we going to open if tons of people start coming here to look for ghosts?"

"Is that why you did it—to protect Simon?" He chuckled but not in a good way. "I wouldn't have thought you'd be someone to impede an investigation. I can see you've changed since we were married."

"Go away," I groaned. "This isn't something that's going to help me or Simon. Go investigate something else."

A breath beside my ear whispered, "What about taking a closer look at the dead man? What about his family? Why was he fighting to keep the book shop from opening? Perhaps it was to lay blame on your friend, as it was a good time to be rid of him?"

A cold breeze shuddered through me, and I shivered.

Daniel saw it and noticed my skimpy attire. "I'm sorry. I shouldn't have come in here guns blazing. Get dressed. Let's talk."

There was a moment when his gaze went over me that I didn't feel cold at all. What was the age for menopause hot flashes? I was barely thirty. Surely this was too soon.

"Sorry. I'll change. I can meet you at the station if you like?"

"No. I'll wait until you come down."

"Okay. I'll be fast." I started up the stairs and felt his eyes follow me. What was wrong with him anyway? What was wrong with me? We were done with this years ago. Why the sudden interest? That was a mystery I wished would go away before I had to solve it.

I showered quickly and changed into good jeans — the ones without holes or paint on them — and a pretty pink top. Looking at myself in the steamy mirror, I put on some lipstick. I did a childish thing and wrote his name in the mist on the mirror. I wiped it off with a towel almost as soon as I did it but not soon enough to keep Dickens from seeing it.

"So that's how it is, eh? It doesn't surprise me. You are a flighty young woman. But if you must harbor a *tendre* for the man, you could at least advance your cause by not dressing as a street boy. A pretty street boy, no doubt, but a boy nonetheless."

"He's waiting," I whispered, not questioning why the ghost was in my bathroom. "Go to sleep or something. I'm trying to get my day organized."

I slipped my feet into my good tennis shoes — no holes or paint — and hurried back downstairs. A marvelous aroma filled the house. I sniffed the air. French toast. I remembered Daniel making that for us when we were together. It was the only food he could cook without a microwave.

"Smells good," I enthused, deciding during my shower that the best way through this was helping him figure out who killed Mr. Hart. He was obviously truthful that he was on Simon's side. I was going to have to trust him on that and hope for the best. "You can still make French toast."

He slid two pieces of egg-soaked bread on my plate and sprinkled them with powdered sugar. "Actually I'm quite a good cook now. I can make all kinds of things without the microwave."

"Thank you. You didn't have to make me breakfast." He poured us both a cup of coffee. "I wouldn't have starved to death while we were talking. How did you find everything, anyway?"

"Simon keeps a tight ship." He sat across from me. "And I notice things. It's part of my job."

I ate a bit of French toast and took a sip of coffee. I would never have believed that Daniel and I would be sitting across a table from each other again and politely eating breakfast. Not in this lifetime. It wasn't that we'd hated each other when we'd split up. It was more just not thinking we'd ever be this close again.

"I think we're looking in the wrong direction," he said. "I'm going to start moving the investigation more into Ebenezer Hart's life. I want to know why he opposed the book shop and more about him personally."

Had he heard what Dickens said to me? What he was saying was almost word for word the same.

"I'm glad you're not investigating Simon anymore. Is it because he was poisoned?"

"Not really. It seemed like the two of you were perfect suspects for the murder. I wanted to make sure you weren't."

I put down my cup with a little more force than was necessary. "What does that mean? You really thought I murdered someone?"

He cut his French toast into miniscule pieces. It was

his way of avoiding a subject while he was eating. I wasn't going to let him get away with it.

"Did you think I killed Ebenezer Hart?"

"No." He finally looked up at me. "The truth? As Deputy Chief, I see all the cases that come in for the Portsmouth Police Department. I saw your name on this one, and I asked if I could take the investigation. I didn't think you were guilty. I wanted to make sure that you didn't get dragged down in this."

That was hard to believe, but he seemed sincere. "Really? You were worried about me after all this time?"

Daniel smiled self-consciously and cleared his throat. "Of course. It's not like I forgot about you or the time we spent together. I can't imagine how long that would take."

"Oh."

"More coffee?" He got to his feet in a quick movement. "More French toast? There are still two pieces left."

"No thanks." I dabbed my lips with a napkin for something to do with my hands. "Well, thank you for caring about me. I'm glad you didn't think I killed Mr. Hart. I hope you realize that Simon didn't either."

He poured himself another cup of coffee and sat down again. "I don't think Simon is involved either, which is why I thought I needed to come at it from another direction. That and my boss yelling at me this morning about the ghost thing in the paper. He threatened to give the case to someone else. I have to solve this, Lisa."

I got up to put my plate and cup in the sink. Since it looked like neither one of us was going to eat the extra

French toast, I put that in a Tupperware container in the refrigerator. If we didn't go shopping soon, it would be the only thing in the house to eat.

A weird thing happened as I came back to the table. The salt shaker seemed to jump off the table and hit the floor on Daniel's side. I stepped in that direction to retrieve it and felt a strong push from behind me.

"Dickens," I muttered and then fell right into Daniel's lap.

Chapter Seventeen

Too Close for Comfort

"Love her. Love her. If she favors you, love her."

I felt sure I heard the ghost laugh. What was he doing now, playing matchmaker?

"Are you all right?" Daniel tried to help me sit up, but even then I was still lying on him. I put my hand up to get off him, but it was squarely in his chest. I moved abruptly and lost my balance again.

"I'm fine," I managed to say with my mouth against his sleeve. "Just an attack of the clumsies, I guess." *Brought on by a ghost-turned-matchmaker.* We were going to have words about this and not the kind that would go in his book.

We finally managed to separate from each other. Daniel put his hands on my waist and helped me to my feet. We stared into each other's eyes, and he whispered my name.

It almost happened. I almost kissed him. He almost kissed me. The world almost went mad.

But before the kiss could happen, I moved away from him. I got off about a dozen apologies as I moved, embarrassed but also excited to be so close to him. I couldn't let that happen again.

"So what exactly are you planning to investigate about Mr. Hart?" I asked as I started to sit in my chair again. It quickly slipped out from under me, no doubt a joke perpetrated by a certain specter. I dropped hard on the wood floor, feeling the smack against my rear end as if someone had spanked me.

Daniel came quickly around the table and helped me up. I ground my teeth in frustration, assuring him that I was fine. Just very embarrassed.

The doorbell rang, and I apologized, going to answer it. Admiral Leazer and Mrs. Tappen were waiting at the door.

"What is the meaning of this?" The Admiral demanded as he smacked his newspaper down on the table next to Daniel's. "It's not enough that you want to put yet another shop in Olde Town. Now you want to make us a laughingstock with this ghost stupidity."

"And the ghost of a venerable author at that." Mrs. Tappen followed the Admiral into the foyer. "It's preposterous! Why would a man like Charles Dickens want to haunt this house? For shame, Miss Wellman. For shame."

"I'd really like to help you with that." I glanced at my watch. "But look at the time. I have to go to the hospital and get Simon. I'm afraid I'll have to ask you to leave now. I'm sure you'll want to come back later and see him."

"And no doubt bring him up to speed on what's been going on here while he's been gone." The Admiral shook his finger at me. "The truth will come out, young woman."

"We need to go." Daniel came to my rescue. "Sorry, folks. We have to get a move on."

I went along with the ruse, letting Daniel do crowd control on the Admiral and Mrs. Tappen.

Once outside with the door locked and the alarm system on, I was fine with taking a taxi to get Simon. "I'll see you later. Let me know if there's anything I can do."

"I'll drop you off," he said. "No point in calling a taxi before you get Simon."

"As soon as he's out of the hospital, I'm going to get the plate renewed on the Bentley. Thanks, Daniel."

"Don't mention it. We can talk about the new plan for finding the killer on the way." He shut the door behind me and got behind the wheel.

Everything was going fine until he asked about the ghost.

"The newspaper account looked a little over-the-top from what I saw," I told him. "The paranormal group that was there promised not to say anything about what they saw."

He glanced at me. "Are you saying you thought it was real?"

"I didn't at first," I told him. "But now I'm not the

only one who's seen Dickens. I feel saner."

"I'm not sure exactly why that is," he said. "Seeing ghosts isn't exactly a normal thing."

"Maybe not normal, but he has a reason for showing up—an agenda like the rest of us."

"And that is?"

"He wants me to help him finish his last novel. He died while he was writing it, and he'd like to see it have the ending he wanted it to have."

Daniel chuckled. "He wants you to help him? I'm assuming because you're a writer too, even though you've never published anything. It seems odd that he wouldn't go to Stephen King or John Grisham, doesn't it?"

"I don't know. Maybe he went to them first, and they turned him down. Or maybe they can't see ghosts. My friend, Dana, from the paranormal group says not everyone can." That last crack had hurt my feelings. Just because I wasn't published didn't mean I wasn't a good writer.

"Yeah, I guess that makes sense."

"What does that mean?" I demanded hotly.

"Come on, Lisa. You can admit to me that this is all some kind of publicity stunt for the book shop opening. It's okay. I get it. My boss isn't happy about it, but I get it."

"That's not true. You can ask Dana. I asked them not to say anything about the ghost. I didn't expect it to be in the newspaper this morning."

"I think your friend let you down. Maybe she thought it was a publicity thing too."

We reached the hospital, and I was happy to get out of the car. This time he didn't offer to come with me. I said goodbye quickly, in case he changed his mind, and walked inside the main annex.

Simon was up, dressed, and ready to go when I got there. We had to wait another hour before the doctor finally released him. The nurses all came in to hug him one last time. I smiled when I saw how popular he was with the ladies. Several of them gave him their phone numbers, and many of those were twenty or thirty years younger than him.

He took it all in stride, smiling and accepting their warmth and hospitality. He was good-looking for an older man and had a way about him that was quite charming. I remembered being the recipient of that dashing charm when he'd come to the library and spoken with me.

That was partly what had convinced me to leave the library. Not because he'd seduced me but because I thought how wonderful he'd be as a book shop owner. I could imagine him welcoming his guests to his home-turned-book shop. I hoped I was right about my investment in the future.

"I am happy to be leaving this establishment," he said as we went down in the elevator. His wheelchair was covered with flowers and cookies that I couldn't hold for carrying all the other gifts he'd received.

"Oh, Simon," the older nurse giggled. "I can't believe you want to leave us."

He smiled at her. "Not you, my dear, but the routine and quite frankly, the antiseptic smell of the place. Not to mention the frequent blood pressure checks. I feel as though my arm will never be the same."

I'd called a taxi from the room when everything

was ready to go. It was waiting out front for us. No sign of Daniel, thank goodness, I told myself as I scanned the parking lot. I certainly didn't want him there.

I put everything I was holding and then everything Simon was holding in the trunk of the taxi. The nurse helped him into the car, and we were ready to go. I took one last look around the parking lot before I got in beside him. What a fool I was to watch for Daniel. He was only there because of Mr. Hart. I had to remind myself of that. This wasn't twelve years ago when I couldn't wait to see him and my heart beat faster when he was near.

The taxi started home. Simon glanced at me. "I'm sorry your young man wasn't there to greet us. I assume he had work. Otherwise I'm sure wild horses couldn't have kept him away."

"I told you, we're divorced. It's been a long time since we broke up. It's not like we have a relationship outside of the murder investigation." I said it to him but was thinking I needed a reminder every few minutes. I'd be glad when this was behind us.

"Yes." He patted my hand. "We all leave something of ourselves in the past, Miss Wellman. It's rare that it can be retrieved."

Instead of answering that since I was already feeling a little weepy, I launched into where we were as far as our anticipated shop opening on the day after Thanksgiving. There were still thousands of books to be put on shelves, and I'd lost count of how many boxes needed to be checked. I went over every detail of where I thought the remaining furniture and accessories should go in the individual rooms.

Simon didn't say a word. I glanced at him—he was sleeping. Another moment and he was snoring.

I felt terrible that I'd forgotten he'd just left the hospital in my eagerness to put Daniel out of my mind. I knew Simon would still feel the effects of having been so ill. He'd need at least another day or two before he'd be fit to get back into putting the book shop together. I patted his hand and took a deep breath. Things would unfold as they did in every plot. I just had to give them time.

As we turned into our neighborhood, the taxi driver slowed down and whistled through his teeth. "What in the world's going on here?"

I looked out of the window, ripped from my reverie, and saw dozens of people in our drive and scattered across the still-green lawn like autumn leaves. All of them had cameras of one kind or another. Some of them had large cameras with TV logos on them.

"What's this, then?" Simon woke to see our guests.

"I'd hoped this wouldn't happen, though I should have known better. I'm sorry. Something happened last night that wasn't supposed to happen, and now everyone wants to know what happened."

He put his hand on my forehead. "Are you quite all right, Miss Wellman? I don't believe I've ever heard anyone use the word happen so many times in one breath. Exactly what did happen?"

I quickly explained, my head down, feeling guilty. "I'm sorry. I should have told you at the hospital, but I was hoping—"

"Yes, yes. I know. Hoping nothing happened, but it obviously did." He gazed out at the small sea of human faces who were staring at us as we waited too long to get out of the taxi. "How perfectly marvelous! Canterville Book Shop and ghosts. What more could anyone ask for?"

"Really?" I peeked at him. "You're not upset?"

"Why in the world would I be upset? I've had to live with the bloody ghosts for the past fifty years. Now I can share them with you, Miss Wellman, and the rest of the reading world. Good combination, wouldn't you say?"

I was completely astounded and couldn't say anything for a moment or two. "You know about Dickens? Has he always been here?"

"Absolutely not. I'm thankful to say that the house has always attracted literary genius but fortunately not him. I am not overly fond of his work. Of course, I am a gracious host to the living or the dead."

"What are you saying?" I squirmed to face him in the backseat. "There have been other ghosts in the house?"

"Meter's running, lady," the driver reminded me.

"Sorry." I turned back to Simon.

"That's okay. If you got the money, I got the time."

"Now. Other ghosts?" I prompted.

"Why yes, of course. Didn't I tell you? How remiss of me. Perhaps we should go inside and discuss it over a cup of tea."

"That sounds like a good idea." But it was much easier said than done.

The crowd on the lawn had grown. As soon as we stepped out of the car, people realized we lived there and began asking questions. I asked the taxi driver to wait while I helped Simon into the house. I had to push my way through them on the way out to get the flowers and cookies out of the trunk. I almost forgot to pay the driver and had to go back for that too.

"We just want to see the ghost of Dickens," a woman said as she shoved against me. "Is he here now? Can we call back Emily Dickinson too?"

I didn't answer as I struggled to get the flowers and cookies to the house. The crowd surrounded me and demanded entrance to the house. I dropped some flowers and bent to get them, but the visitors beat me to it and held them up as some kind of souvenir. I would have dropped everything else just to get into the house, but Bob Stanhope, Simon's lawyer, was suddenly there and helped me get through the crowd with Simon's things.

"Thanks," I said when we were inside. "I can't believe so many people want to see the ghost of Charles Dickens."

He put cookies and flowers on the table by the door. "That happens sometimes when the media picks up on what's going on." He thrust his steely gaze at me. "What *is* going on, Miss Wellman?"

Simon was in the kitchen and heard Bob. "Come in for tea," he said. "We can talk. Miss Wellman, can you locate those delightful shortbread cookies Nurse Angela gave me? They were delectable."

Bob joined Simon, and I found the cookies. The box was open, and I wanted to eat all of them. Stress always made me crave sweets. I'd fought it all my life with different levels of success. This wasn't one of those times as I ate one of the cookies on my way to the dining room where Simon and Bob were getting tea together.

"What a mess out there," Bob said as he sat at the

table. "I read the article in the paper this morning, but I agree with Miss Wellman. Who would've thought that many people would believe in something like this?"

"Ghosts are always a draw," Simon said. "Here's your tea, Miss Wellman. I see you found the cookies."

I shared the box, even though I didn't want to. He was right. The cookies were amazing.

"Is that why you called?" Bob sneered at the idea of eating a cookie.

More for me—I snagged two of them and put them on my saucer.

"Actually, I called because recent events have shown me that I need to rethink my life. Or my death, as it were. We've spoken of this before, and you talked me into waiting. But no more." Simon helped himself to cookies.

Bob took out his briefcase. "What is it you want me to do?"

"I'd like you to change my will and leave Miss Wellman as the heir to this wonderful, old house. I believe she'll do it justice."

Chapter Eighteen

A Confession

"You have been the last dream of my soul."

"What?" I asked with cookie in my mouth. Part of it fell on the table, and I quickly snatched it up. "What are you saying, Simon?"

"You heard me," he replied firmly. "You know I dislike chewing my cabbage twice."

Bob cleared his throat. "We've talked about this since you met Miss Wellman. You still barely know her. Think of your son, Simon. It's not fair to leave this valuable piece of real estate to someone outside the family."

"I am thinking of my son," he replied. "Ashcroft isn't interested in the house except to sell it. He has no notion of how to run a book shop nor would he want to. He also doesn't understand ghosts — a thing I didn't realize about Miss Wellman until this morning. It solidifies my position on the matter. I want someone to have it that will carry on its marvelous legacy."

My head felt like it was spinning. I hadn't said or done anything that would put me in this position. I didn't want to interfere with Ashcroft's inheritance. Goodness knew how much he'd despise me if he found out. And by the look on Bob's face, he'd tell him as soon as he could.

"I appreciate the offer, Simon," I told him. "But I don't want you to leave me the house. It's enough that I get to be your partner in starting the book shop. I don't need anything else."

Simon looked down his aristocratic nose at me. "Do keep quiet, Miss Wellman. I am taking care of the future of this house. We'll talk later. Perhaps you should begin shelving books again."

He'd never spoken to me that way. I was hurt, and curious, as to why he did it. But I played along and left the room. I didn't go far, just into the parlor where I shelved books, still listening to the discussion between Simon and Bob.

Bob did the best he could to dissuade Simon from changing his will. He had very convincing arguments. But in the end, Simon knew what he wanted. Bob agreed to draw up the papers and gave me a hard look on his way out of the house. I closed the door behind him after a quick look outside at the ever-growing crowd. Then I went to find Simon.

He'd retired to his room and lay on his bed. I knocked at the doorway and asked if he was all right.

"I'm fine. A tad tired, but I'll get over it."

"Why did you do it?" I sat in the heavy, green chenille-upholstered chair closest to the bed. "Why did you change your will? And why did you talk to me like that in front of Bob?"

He sighed and pushed himself up on the bed. "It is rare to find a kindred spirit in this world, Miss Wellman. My dear Ariadne was as much a part of me as I was of her. When we moved here before Ashcroft was born, we moved with more books than furniture. We both loved to read, you see."

"So you see me as a kindred spirit." I nodded. "I feel the same about you. But giving me the house is too much. Ashcroft is going to be furious."

"Which matters less to me than a drop of rain on an azalea." He dismissed the idea with his hand. "One of the first things that Ariadne and I learned about this house was that it was haunted by the spirits of authors who had gone before. I had hoped you would witness these phenomena. I can't tell you how pleased I was this morning to hear you say so."

"Simon—"

"However, I made this decision before I knew of your propensity to see the spirits." He chuckled. "I don't want Ashcroft destroying everything we are building here. There must be books here for the spirits to continue. I knew a book shop would take care of the problem, and I knew you were the right one to do it."

"I don't know what to say."

"I do apologize for speaking to you so roughly. But you have the disposition of a bulldog when it comes to understanding what's going on. I didn't want to say this to you in front of Bob. He certainly would have no belief in the ghosts who abide here. Forgive me."

"Of course." I was stunned by his words. "So other authors have haunted this house?"

"Oh, yes. What a delight it has been to host such remarkable writers as Rudyard Kipling, William Shakespeare, and Jane Austen."

"Shakespeare?" I could feel my eyes grow wide with his admission.

"So you understand why it is essential for this house to continue with too many books in it?"

"Yes, I do. I'm just not sure—"

He closed his eyes and slid back down on the bed. "I apologize that I must rest now. We shall discuss this matter further later."

I walked out of the room in a daze. Ghosts of authors were here all the time? It wasn't just a one-time thing? Had I died and gone to heaven?

Dickens was nowhere to be found. I spent an entire hour looking for him and finally gave up. I needed to spend time getting the books shelved. Also on my list was a visit from someone who'd bought all of Simon's extra furnishings. They were coming to pick them up. I just hoped they could get through the crowd.

Twice while I was working, someone knocked at the door, and I thought it was the junk man. Instead it was a ghost fanatic who wanted to see Charles Dickens. I got calls from two television stations that I hoped I could put off until the store opened. This was valuable publicity but not just yet.

But if I played it right, I could see where the book shop could have a truly grand opening after

Thanksgiving.

I spent the rest of the morning shelving books before looking up and realizing it was lunch time. I cleaned up — some of the books were dusty — and went to rouse Simon to ask what he wanted to eat.

"It is my fervent hope that we have solid food, Miss Wellman," he said. "I have had enough soup and applesauce to last me a good long while. My teeth long for the feel of meat on them."

Sometimes Simon's descriptiveness went a little too far.

"Well, I could make some toast. And there are crackers. I haven't been able to get out to shop. I didn't realize the Bentley needed a new license plate. Daniel pointed that out to me, and now I feel like he's watching to see if I drive it."

"Whatever you have will suffice," he said. "I shall summon the mechanic who will take care of your distress and my need for meat."

I made some scrambled eggs and toast with some tomatoes on the side. The tea was ready by the time the food was finished. I found some trifle left from a few days ago. It smelled fine, so I scooped it into dishes and put it on the table.

We had barely sat down to eat when the front door opened, and Ashcroft came inside. I knew Bob would waste no time telling him about losing his inheritance.

"I demand an explanation," he said after fighting off the crowd trying to rush in. "What's going on in the yard? And why is Miss Wellman to inherit my house?"

Simon laughed. "Your house? Surely you mean my house. I'm not dead yet, my boy."

"Don't mince words with me, Father." Ashcroft put

his hands behind his back and paced the floor. "You've taken up with this floozy, and she's getting everything you own."

"I was going to ask you if you wanted lunch," I steamed. "But the floozy thinks you can take care of yourself."

"Not that I care to eat at the table with *you*," he continued.

"You're still getting the bulk of my estate, Ashcroft. There's no reason to mope about not having the house. You already have a fine house of your own. You don't need this one."

"I didn't mean I wanted to live here. But selling the old place would bring a pretty penny." Ashcroft actually rubbed his hands together at this point.

Stabbing a piece of egg, I realized that I could easily hate him.

"That's exactly why you won't inherit it," Simon told him. "I even added something to the will so that if Miss Wellman passes without naming an heir, it will go to a foundation to keep books in the house."

Wordsworth started barking, or at least trying to. Puck jumped up in the air and flipped over backwards before running to the kitchen door to get away from the noise. Truffles continued grooming herself in the corner, and Maggie May indolently stared at the ceiling.

"A foundation?" Ashcroft demanded. "You'd actually rather give this house to a book foundation than see me get it? I didn't realize that you hated me so much."

"I don't hate you." Simon shook his head. "You are a bit melodramatic. You take after your mother's side of the family in that way, I fear. But I have spoken with her, and she agrees that you aren't the right person for the house."

Ashcroft stared at me. "Now he's talking to my mother, who's been dead for ten years. What's next? Don't think this will has a chance to hold up in court, Miss Wellman. The house will belong to me."

He had the same fight getting out of the house around the ghost hunters that he had getting in. I didn't feel sorry for him about the house now that I understood why it was important that books had to remain here. But I did understand his anger over the situation.

"Shall we finish lunch?" Simon asked. "Don't look so stricken. Ashcroft grew up here but never experienced a spirit sighting. It may have been because he has never enjoyed reading. I don't know where Ariadne and I went wrong."

"Are you really speaking with your dead wife?" I asked carefully. Why would I think it was any stranger than me speaking with Dickens?

"Yes." He gazed at me across the table. "She likes you. Did I mention that Ariadne was an author? Yes. She published three books in her lifetime. They were all remarkable works. The house welcomed her, as do I."

An author? "Are her books here?"

"Yes, of course. I'll show you. She wrote the most wonderful prose."

After he'd pointed out her books—all three, romances set in Europe—we both shelved books. Around three, there was another knock on the door. This time it was the junk man, or woman, in this case.

She was about my age with flyaway brown hair,

blue eyes, and a wonderful tan for November. She held out her hand with an amazing smile, like a model or an actress. "Hi. I'm Dae O'Donnell from Missing Pieces Thrift Shop. I'm here to pick up the load Simon Canterville called about."

"Hello. I'm Lisa Wellman, Simon's partner. We have everything out back. I'll take you there."

"Thanks." She waved to a man in an older, red pickup truck, showing him that he needed to drive around the back of the house.

Simon walked out the back door with Puck at his ankles. "Dae O'Donnell! So good to see you. How is your shop doing? How is Duck faring these days? And who is this young man replacing Horace?"

Dae hugged him. "Everything is fine. This is my fiancé, Kevin Brickman. He runs the Blue Whale Inn. Gramps is okay but busy. Our police chief had a heart attack, and he's taken over his job for a while."

"Pleased to meet you, sir." Kevin shook his hand.

"Very pleased to meet you as well." Simon enthusiastically shook back. "Thank you for coming. You were the only one I'd trust with these things to make sure they get to the right people who will love them as much as Ariadne and I did."

Dae glanced into the garage and then up at the back of the house. "What happened that you're getting rid of them, Simon? I know you love these pieces."

"Best come inside, and I'll show you around. Would you like some tea? Miss Wellman, put the kettle on."

While I cleared breakfast and got set up for tea, Simon took Kevin and Dae through the transformed Victorian and told them all our plans for the book shop.

I knew he must trust them to do so. He was reluctant to talk to most people about it.

When they came back downstairs, we sat down at the rosewood table. Dae held Simon's hand and closed her eyes. "I knew you seemed pale," she said. "Someone tried to poison you. Are you all right?"

"Yes, dear. I'm fine. Don't worry. Miss Wellman has taken quite good care of me."

"But how did it happen?" she asked. "I can see it wasn't an accident."

I drew in a sharp breath. "Really? How do you know?"

She smiled as she put multiple lumps of sugar in her cup. "The same way I saw Charles Dickens hiding among your bookshelves. I have the sight."

Chapter Nineteen

The Harridan

"'Tis love that makes the world go round, my baby."

"The sight?" I managed to spill my tea and wiped it up quickly. "Have you always had it? What can you see?"

"Everything," Kevin assured me, no sugar in his tea. "Trust me. She sees everything."

Simon laughed. "It's true. And she's had the gift since she was a small child. Ariadne and I used to visit the Outer Banks regularly to see the horses and get away for a few days. We even stayed at the Blue Whale Inn once before it closed. Nice to know it's open again.

Perhaps I'll come for a visit once we get the book shop going."

"That's incredible." I offered the meager platter of tea snacks I could put together without shopping. If people continued to stop by before the license was on the Bentley, there wouldn't be any food at all.

"Confound it all." Dickens charged into the room, making the chandelier in the foyer sway and the curtains on the windows blow as if they were all open to a brisk sea breeze. "It is bloody well annoying. A man deserves his privacy. No ghost needs people peeking in on him."

Dae, Simon, and I all laughed. Kevin shook his head and sipped his tea.

"You can't see or hear him, can you?" I asked.

"No. But that's okay," he said. "I leave that stuff to Dae."

"I don't think I could see anything like this until I moved here," I confided. "Something about this house. It's scary and awesome."

"I'm sure you'll pick up on more than a few stories from my things," Simon said to Dae. "If anything interesting turns up, be sure to call. Ariadne and I would be thrilled to hear any history we didn't already know."

"I'll do that."

She obviously knew them well enough to be aware that Simon's wife was dead. But she didn't act strange at all about the idea that he would share information about the furniture with her.

We talked for thirty minutes or so until Dae and Kevin were ready to leave. I walked with them back out to the garage. It would be great to get my Beetle out once this stuff was gone. I helped them load everything in the back of the pickup.

"What's with the protesters out front?" Kevin asked as he worked.

"They aren't protesters." I sighed over a beautiful, blue, art deco vase as I put it in a box in the back of the truck. "I made a mistake and invited some friends who are interested in paranormal research to the house. They swore they wouldn't talk to the media after seeing Dickens, but you can see how that worked out."

"Take good care of Simon," Dae said. "I still feel that he's in danger. Do you know who poisoned him?"

"I don't like saying it, but I think it might have been his son, Ashcroft. Simon wants the house to stay as a book shop even after his death. Ashcroft was a little eager to go through Simon's things after he was in custody and even told him he'd sell the house."

"I'm sure he didn't like that. I hope it wasn't Ashcroft," Dae said. "I'd hate that to be the case. I'd be willing to take a look at whatever poisoned him so I could add something useful to finding who did it."

"I wish I could do that, but the police have the bottle of lavender oil."

"Well, good luck." She hugged me too. "Be careful. And don't worry about Dickens. The ghosts here only stay a while. They're temporary guests — until the next visitor."

"Next visitor?"

Kevin laughed. "Goodbye, Lisa. Come visit us sometime."

I watched them leave before getting my Beetle out of the garage. It was wonderful to be back in my own car again. I hadn't realized how much I missed it.

Everything was so close in Olde Town that I could walk almost everywhere. But the last few days had shown me that sometimes I needed a car. Better mine than the Bentley. I made sure to pull it on the side where it would be out of the way and yet accessible.

"Dae is a wonderful woman, isn't she?" Simon mentioned as he cleaned up after tea.

"She's very nice." I took the two cups from him. "I'll take care of this. You're supposed to be resting."

"Pish. That's all I did in the hospital. I'm ready to put more books on the shelves."

But I convinced him to sit down with one of his favorite books, *John Carter of Mars*. I could see by the dog-eared pages of the book how much he enjoyed it. On his nightstand was a more recent author — Mary Higgins Clark. He enjoyed mysteries as much as I did. I knew that from our visits at the library.

"I'll read for an hour," he said. "Then I'll be ready to put more books away. We don't have much time, you know, Miss Wellman. We'll be open for business before you know it."

There was a small place for reading, two chairs and a table, in each room. There was also one room that only had a few books and several places to sit and read. That was the front parlor where we would also have bags and wrapping paper. I figured the tablet could go anywhere in the house to take orders or allow customers to pay for books. Of course that was if I could convince Simon not to have one of those large, ornate cash registers that he loved so much. I supposed it could just be another antique if it had to. We wouldn't have to use it.

As I walked through the rooms, I thought how

wonderful it would be if we could serve tea and coffee each day. Maybe we could have a station for it in the front parlor. There would be doors between the kitchen and dining room separating our living space from the open areas for customers. I'd have to talk to Simon about the idea, but I was sure he would love it.

I glanced out the front window. The crowds of ghost lovers were still there. Some had brought chairs and bottles of soda. There were already wrapping papers from candy bars and hamburgers. It was going to be a mess to clean up.

Mrs. Tappen came up the sidewalk, ignoring the people around her, walking at her normal, brisk speed. She was wearing her usual power suit, green, her bright blond hair artfully curled. As I watched she tried to use a key to open the door. It wouldn't open since the locks had been changed.

She knocked at the door and waited impatiently with her foot tapping on the porch floor.

"Good morning." I reached the ground floor. "Would you like to come in?"

"No, I would not." She leveled one of her annoyed glances at me. "Where is Simon? I need to speak with him."

"He's resting. He just got home from the hospital, you know. Maybe he could call you later."

She pushed me aside as she bustled into the foyer and the front parlor. "That's all right. I'll find him. You just go about your business."

As I had several times before, I wondered about Mrs. Tappen and Simon. He'd been a widower for ten years. I wasn't sure how long her husband had been dead. I thought there might be something personal between them, something more intimate, though the idea made me gag a little.

Still, she knew her way around the house and had a key. Maybe she was just a good neighbor. But what about Ariadne? If her ghost was still here, would he mess around with Mrs. Tappen in front of her?

Even though he was just home from the hospital, I decided Simon was an adult and didn't need my protection from the woman. He knew her well, it seemed. But I really wanted to hear what she had to say and ended up following her to the main reading room where Simon was. I could hear her voice as I went up the stairs.

"You've made us a laughingstock, Simon," she complained. "It wasn't bad enough that you wanted to put a book shop here. Now we're going to be on that ghastly ghost tour of haunted houses. How will I ever sell another house in this area? You know people who want to live in Olde Town are sophisticated and well-heeled. They don't have time to drive around groups of hysterical individuals looking for their dead relatives."

He didn't say anything. I glanced into the room and put my hand over my mouth so I wouldn't laugh when I realized that he was sound asleep. He hadn't heard a thing that she'd said. Not that I thought he cared, since he enjoyed the notion of ghosts being here. He wouldn't want to make ghost tours our main attraction, but he also wouldn't care about her harangue.

"Simon?" She shook him a little. He didn't respond. "Simon!" She shook him harder and punched him in the arm. "Are you really asleep, or are you ignoring me?"

"I'm sorry." He coughed as though he had been asleep, rubbing his eyes and yawning. "What did you say? Oh, Mrs. Tappen. How pleasant to see you here."

She punched him again, and I decided that was enough, even if it was his personal business. She knew he'd been ill. Not that I thought she should have punched him even if he was well. She'd probably left a bruise.

"Allow me to rid you of the harridan," Dickens whispered from my left side.

I hadn't seen him there and was startled enough to jump. "All right. But don't hurt her. She could sue us."

He bowed his head slightly in response, but I could see the devilish look in his eyes.

Was it the right thing to do? I wasn't sure, and it was too late. The curtains at the windows fluttered, and the small chandelier above them swayed.

"What's going on?" Mrs. Tappen demanded. "I don't believe in your ghost tricks, Simon. You know that. Do you plan to scare your customers into buying these smelly, old books?"

"I have no notion of why this is happening." He looked across the room at me. "Miss Wellman, are you responsible?"

The beautiful, turquoise oriental carpet in the middle of the floor began spinning. We planned to set a large table there to display some books, but we hadn't done it yet thankfully. The carpet was free to lift up from the floor and take a short journey around the room a few times before settling back down.

"I'm sorry, Simon. I don't have anything to do with it." But my sincere apology was ruined when I saw the look on Mrs. Tappen's face. She was angry and afraid.

"That's it," she said. "I've tried to help you. I've tried to be your friend, Simon. But I'm through with you. Don't look for my assistance when you need it."

She stormed by me again, nearly pushing me over in her haste to get out of the room. I heard her march down the first flight of stairs and slam the door behind her.

"Dickens, eh?" Simon chuckled. "The man is a prankster, by God."

"Not surprising from his writing," I said. "Well, except for his later works, but he was under duress."

"So true. And sometimes Mrs. Tappen is enough to make anyone under duress." He got up and put down his book. "But you were right, Miss Wellman. I feel wonderfully refreshed after that brief nap. Time to get back to work."

The mechanic came for the Bentley. Simon had the saddest look on his face when the man told him he couldn't have it back until the next day.

"Bother," Simon remarked when he was gone. "I apologize for the lack of food. We could stroll down to the nearest bistro or order in some quaint ethnic food. A young woman such as yourself needs more than tea and crackers for dinner."

"I got my car out of the garage after Dae and Kevin left. I could take it shopping and get supplies. We don't have to depend on the Bentley for everything."

As we tried to make that decision, Dana and her crew of ghost hunters stopped by. They apologized for the media leak, blaming it on Becky, who had apparently been completely unnerved by the situation.

"Can you believe she'd never seen a real ghost?" Tommy laughed as he stood in the foyer with his hands in his jean pockets.

Dana was more sober about it. "I'm so sorry, Lisa. I had no idea she'd do something like this. Lucky she didn't have all the pictures and data. She only had the information from her phone. But I guess that was enough."

"Would you like us to clear the area or something?" Tommy offered. "It's a mess out there. Maybe the police would come and take care of it. They're trespassing."

"It's not a great time for us, but I don't want to alienate a bunch of potential readers either," I told them. "I hope they all come back when the shop opens."

"We can at least clean the yard," Darren said. "It looks like a trash heap out there."

I thanked him for offering. I certainly wasn't going to turn down the help and gave them trash bags.

"Is he here?" Dana whispered when the two men had gone back outside. "Dickens, I mean. Have you seen him today?"

"Yes." I told her about what happened with Mrs. Tappen. "It was really funny."

"Do you know how unusual it is for a ghost to interact with humans? Mostly they just do what they're going to do and ignore everyone around them. You are *so* lucky. I can't wait to tell the writing group tonight. Maybe you should seriously think about adding a ghost to the book you're working on."

"I suppose it could go with the story." I considered the idea. "Thanks."

"Don't mention it." Her eyes were fierce when she spoke. "Just wait until I see Becky again. I'm not ever taking her out on another mission. I'll have to find another psychic. Usually we need them to get the ghost's attention."

She asked if she could come back and wander around when the book shop was open. I said that was fine as long as she bought some books. The ghost was a nice side effect, but the idea was to sell enough books to stay open.

Dana left a few minutes later. I noticed she didn't help pick up trash, but Darren and Tommy got everything that was out on the ground. They even took the trash with them. I wasn't complaining.

Simon finally made the decision that we should go out to eat, despite the people in the yard.

I changed clothes since I had to before the meeting anyway. I dug out a matching pair of white dress pants and a sweater with seed pearls at the neck. He changed into a gray suit that I thought might have been worn when someone was almost out of mourning. I'd never seen him wear a modern suit, but that was part of his charm.

We walked down to a sandwich shop, leaving the house through the back door after I'd fed Truffles, Maggie May, and Wordsworth. Puck meowed at the door to get out. I knew he'd be hungry later.

There was a brisk wind blowing, sending hundreds of leaves flying down from the trees. A few people were putting up Christmas decorations, and the smell of something wonderful baking filled our senses as we walked.

"Baked apple." Simon sniffed. "With plenty of cinnamon and a touch of nutmeg."

I took a sniff too. "I think that's pumpkin. Unless

the apple has a crust on it. I'm definitely smelling crust."

He smiled and held his face up to the golden beams of sunlight filtering through the trees. "It's wonderful being home and happy. I believe we will make our deadline, Miss Wellman. And as such, I have a marvelous surprise."

"What's that?" I asked glad to see him in such good spirits.

"I ordered the cash register today." He puffed out his narrow chest. "We shall not open without it. The owner of the company has assured me that it will be delivered sometime next week."

"That's wonderful, Simon," I lied. "But we have no idea how to use it."

"I also procured lessons from this man on how to operate this wonderful piece of usable art."

"Great." I smiled, knowing I would still use the tablet. We would only be able to take credit cards with the tablet. But if the cash register made Simon this happy, who was I to argue?

We were lucky and got a table by the window so we could watch traffic and people going by. There were two cars with trees tied on top. That reminded me — we needed a Christmas tree for our grand opening. I hoped Simon had ornaments and other accessories. If not, we might have to make some to stay under budget.

It was a wonderful meal with plenty of shared excitement about the shop. At least until I saw Daniel approach. Lucky we were almost done eating. We could easily leave as he came inside. I hoped it might even be possible that we could get out without him seeing us at all, but that didn't happen.

"Hello, Mr. Canterville." He nodded to me. "Hello, Miss Wellman."

Simon got to his feet. "That's doing it a bit brown, isn't it, Detective? Miss Wellman has told me of your shared history. You must call her by her Christian name."

Daniel smiled. "All right. Hello, Lisa. How are the two of you this evening?"

"We are quite spectacular," Simon proclaimed. "What brings you by, sir? Have you news to share about Mr. Hart or the person who poisoned me?"

"I do, in fact, have some news. May I sit?"

"Of course. Have something to eat. I can recommend the hot turkey with mashed potatoes and a touch of cranberry sauce. It was quite good."

"Thanks," Daniel said. "I'll just have some coffee. I'll be right back."

As soon as he was gone, Simon began pinching my cheeks.

"What are you doing?"

"I know you are a woman of little artifice, Miss Wellman. You must play up what you have in hopes of winning back your husband. Straighten those shoulders. Open your eyes wide. You'll be able to get his attention and perhaps hold it this time. Have you a lipstick in your pocketbook?"

"Stop it." I swatted his hands away. "I don't want to get him back."

"Who are you trying to get back, Lisa?" Daniel asked as he joined us with his coffee.

Chapter Twenty

Hark the Herald Angels Sing

"Life is made of ever so many partings welded together."

I just knew Simon would blurt out what he'd just told me, but surprisingly, he kept it to himself. That left me to fumble with something that sounded reasonable.

"Yes. Our waiter. I'd like some pie." It sounded silly, but it worked. Daniel even hailed the waiter for me.

The pie arrived. Simon had a fresh cup of tea. I hoped the conversation would easily divert to whatever Daniel wanted to tell us. I didn't know what made Simon think Daniel and I would ever be together again. I needed to make sure he understood that it wasn't going to happen.

"I got a lead on the store that sold the lavender oil. It was right here in Olde Town at an herb shop. Technically lavender oil isn't restricted," he said. "Thousands of people use it without any problem. But the doctor at the hospital told me that you showed signs of being allergic to it, besides the fact that it isn't supposed to be ingested."

"Maybe that's why you don't like the way it smells." I smiled at Simon.

"Curious how the mind works," he said. "I once discovered I was allergic to chocolate in much the same way. Were there any fingerprints on the bottle which might reveal my attacker?"

"No. It looked as though the oil had spilled on the outside of the bottle and anything on the glass was smudged and useless." Daniel sat forward and studied Simon's face. "Who knew you might have an issue with lavender?"

"Does that really matter since he wasn't supposed to have it poured down his throat after getting hit in the head?"

"It might," Daniel responded. "You knew he didn't like lavender. That's how you discovered it shouldn't be there. Who else knew?"

"My son, of course," Simon said. "But I can't believe Ashcroft would attempt to kill me. He might want to kill Miss Wellman—but not me."

"He'd want to kill her because the two of you are opening the book shop together?"

"No. Because I've seen fit to make her my heir for the book shop."

Daniel glanced at me suspiciously. "Really? That's not too bad for someone you've only known a few weeks. What do you think that house is worth?"

"It isn't the value of the place that matters, Detective. Ashcroft has no idea what to do with it, and Miss Wellman does."

"Yeah, I could see where that would make you unpopular."

"And I've known Simon for years," I argued. "He and I just started working together."

"Oh, I see." He turned to Simon again. "Anyone else? Any other family members or close friends who might have thought poisoning you with lavender was a good idea?"

"No, of course not."

"Since you don't think your son did it, who do you think was responsible, Mr. Canterville?"

"I have no idea. I hoped you would find out." Daniel started to speak again, and Simon held up his hand. "I am afraid I must leave you briefly. Where was the gentleman's room again?"

I pointed toward the restrooms. Daniel and I sat silently for a moment after Simon left.

"I thought you said you didn't think I killed Mr. Hart?" I asked.

"I don't."

"So you don't think the two events are tied together?"

"I didn't say that either." He glanced toward the direction Simon had gone. "I feel like he's hiding something. Maybe you can talk to him and persuade him to give up whoever he's covering for."

"You mean Ashcroft? I really don't think Simon

believes his son would hurt him. There must be someone else."

"Maybe so, but I can't find anyone who knows him that well. This was a personal attack. The killer came into the house, brought a poison he felt sure Simon might find deadly, and used it on him in his bedroom. That says someone close to him was involved."

"That makes sense. But Simon doesn't really have a lot of people in his life. I don't know what to tell you."

"Just think about it, huh? Get him to think about it too." He glanced at his watch. "I'm meeting with Mr. Hart's law partner in a few minutes. His wife didn't have any answers as to why he might be on your roof. His finances check out just fine. There was no debt, no real reason he'd oppose the book shop. Maybe it was something personal. I'll let you know."

"Thanks."

"Watch your back, Lisa. If Ashcroft is the killer, he could be coming after you next."

Simon wandered across the restaurant as Daniel left. It was time for me to go too, if I was going to the writer's meeting. We were ready, anyway. I had the waiter box the pie and took it with me.

It was getting dark as we started back. The dry leaves crackled under our feet on the sidewalk. A group of people sang Christmas carols — they seemed to be practicing for an event. People walked their dogs, and jingle bells rang. All we needed was a dusting of snow to make it seem like the holiday was closer than it really was.

I was in no hurry for it. Between this being my first Christmas without my mother and fighting for time to get the book shop open, it could wait.

At the door to Simon's house, I left him as he was ready to go inside. "I meet with the writers tonight. Will you be all right alone?"

He bent and gently kissed my hand. "I am never alone, my dear. Enjoy yourself."

Barry Parker hosted the writer's meetings. He was the only one in the group with a large enough place for the big months. Sometimes friends brought friends, and the group expanded. But we had a core group of about ten people who were always there. That included me, Barry, Dana, Doug, Lynette, Wynn, Dottie, Ben, Carrie, and Rosemary.

Barry's house was closer to the library and my mother's house than it was to Simon's place. I drove the Beetle over there and found a tiny spot for it in the driveway. The house was all decked out for Christmas, the entire front covered in thousands of tiny, white lights. Reindeer frolicked on the frosty lawn around an empty sleigh. Santa must have been waiting on the roof.

His wife, Gina, was always there to greet everyone at the door. She wasn't interested in writing, but she was a reader and enjoyed listening to us talk. We all used her as a sounding board for ideas. Sometimes she even became a beta reader for people lucky enough to complete a manuscript. Not to mention that she made a tasty cheese dip.

"Hi, Lisa." She hugged me as I came in. "How'd the move go? I've heard a lot about Simon Canterville since you got there. First a dead man on the roof and then crazy ghost people in your yard. How are you holding up?"

"I'm fine." I gave her my brightest smile, thinking

about Dae O'Donnell's smile. "It's been a crazy couple of weeks. I'm hoping we can still get the book shop opened by the day after Thanksgiving."

"That's ambitious," she returned. "If I can do anything to help, let me know."

"I'll help too." Barry hugged me. "I guess we can start meeting at your book shop once it's ready."

"We could," I agreed. "Or at least take turns, if you want to keep your stranglehold on the group."

He laughed and put his arm around my shoulders as we walked into his den. "Dana was already regaling us with ghost stories about your haunted house. I'm looking forward to seeing it."

"Not me," Carrie said from her spot near the fireplace. "I grew up with people making jokes about my name—thanks, Stephen King—I don't do paranormal."

The rest of the group was eager to pay a visit to the book shop, and I spent the first few minutes talking about everything Simon and I had done getting set up. The only thing writers might like better than writing books was hanging around in book stores—after all, our love of reading is what made us want to write.

While we talked, Dottie and Ben came in, the last of the core group. It appeared we wouldn't have any visitors that night. That was okay with me. I had a lot to talk about.

Dana did too, as she passed around her pictures of Dickens' ghost. "It was the most amazing thing that's ever happened to me. I've seen some spooky stuff, but this was so real."

"Real enough to bring the press to your door, huh, Lisa?" Lynette spooned some cheese dip on her

Christmas plate.

I sipped my hot cider. "Yes. And I hope they'll want to come back and buy books later because right now they're a pain in the butt."

"Enough about the woo-woo stuff." Rosemary had brought printed copies of her new short story. "I need volunteers, besides Gina, who's already read it. Anyone? Or do I start assigning it?"

"I'll take a copy," Doug said.

"Me too." Ben took one from her.

"What about you, Lisa?" Rosemary skewered me with her intense gaze. She wore strange, blue contacts that always made me shiver looking into her eyes. "I read the beginning of your book a few months back."

"I'll take one," I said. "But I'm not sure I'll get to read it before the next meeting. I'm kind of swamped right now."

She plopped one of the copies in my hands. "I'm sure you can find time. Or give it to Dickens. I'd love to know his thoughts on it."

It was clear that Rosemary would be good at the thing most writers dread — promoting their work. She had no problem with that at all.

"I'll do the best I can," was all I could promise.

"So does anyone else have something they want to have read or critiqued?" Barry was our unofficial president and kept the meetings moving. The doorbell rang, and Gina raced to answer it. "If not, we have a special guest tonight. I know you guys love the hands-on stuff."

"Yeah," Wynn agreed. "That visit from the gun shop owner a few months back was awesome. It totally changed the weapon I was planning to use in my novel."

"How's that going?" I asked.

He shrugged. "Not so well. I had to scrap it. But I found a new character I like a lot. I could use the gun for him."

"That's what I was thinking when I happened to meet our guest tonight," Barry replied. "I was thrilled when he said he'd come talk to us even though he didn't have much time to prepare. I want to introduce the City of Portsmouth Deputy Chief of Police, Daniel Fairhaven."

Gina grinned and handed Daniel a glass of hot cider. Everyone else was excited, applauding a little like he was an entertainer.

I kept my seat and barely acknowledged him when we were introduced. I hadn't been with the group long enough for them to know that we'd been married. What was he doing there? I felt like he was stalking me or something. What did he expect to learn about the case in a small writer's group?

"Good evening," Daniel said. "I've never spoken to a writer's group before. I'm willing to answer whatever questions you have."

"What exactly does the Deputy Chief do?" Rosemary asked.

"Mostly I work as a liaison for Chief Masterson. I also have some jurisdiction over investigations and making sure the police department runs smoothly."

Questions from everyone else came fast and furiously. It was easy to understand why Daniel had his position. He was smooth and quick with answers. He looked everyone in the eye as he spoke and was friendly and helpful.

Of course I knew all those things about him. I scanned Rosemary's short story while he spoke to keep from looking at him. I found four misspelled words in the first paragraph.

Was Daniel following me? Nothing else made any sense. This group was really small and not on anyone's database. What would be the chance that he would just run into Barry and show up here tonight?

But what did that mean? Was Daniel interested in me personally again? Or did he think I was a suspect in Mr. Hart's murder, even though he said I wasn't? It didn't make any sense to me.

"Lisa!"

"Yes?" Barry had to call my name twice before I heard him. I could feel Daniel staring at me and refused to stare back.

"Don't you have any questions for Mr. Fairhaven?"

"Oh. Sorry. I was reading Rosemary's story. It was totally riveting."

"Really?" Rosemary perked up. "What did you like best about it?"

"Ladies." Barry recalled our attention. "We have a guest who's giving us valuable information we can use in our stories. Maybe we could talk about Rosemary's stuff later."

I had no choice but to look at Daniel. He had a knowing expression on his handsome face. Whatever the reason, he was there because I was there. Either he was worried about me or he was keeping an eye on me.

Either idea made me nervous.

Chapter Twenty-one

Too little too late?

"There is nothing so strong or safe in an emergency of life as the simple truth."

There was only one question I wanted to ask our guest, and that had to wait until we got outside. I didn't want to drag the rest of the group into our discussion.

I waited for Daniel by his car while he said his goodbyes and gave out business cards in case my friends had any questions later. He actually looked surprised to see me when he walked out of the house.

"Nice group," he said. The night had grown colder

and his breath was frosty.

"Why were you here? You had to go out of your way to do this. Don't lie to me—why did you invade my writing group?"

"It wasn't out of my way. I talk to groups all the time. It's part of my job."

The light from the house and the Christmas decorations came from behind him. I couldn't see his face, but I knew he was lying.

"I don't believe you. You're here for a specific reason. Are you afraid for me? Or are you afraid I'll kill someone?"

"Don't be so dramatic," he casually replied. "It really was one of those serendipity moments. I had no idea you were a member of this group. How would I know?"

"You looked into it. It wouldn't be that hard to do. We have a website. Don't talk down to me, Daniel. Tell me the truth."

He glanced toward the house, but we were still the only ones who had left. "Okay. I'm worried about Ashcroft Canterville. I don't understand why he would kill Ebenezer Hart, but I get why he might want his father dead, and that reasoning extends to you too."

"So you thought he'd try to kill me at my writer's meeting. That doesn't make any sense. I don't believe Ashcroft would try to kill me." But I opened my car door so I could glance in the backseat, even though Ashcroft would have to fold himself in half to hide there. I thought I might as well take advantage of him while he was standing there.

"Suit yourself," he said. "But I know you better than that. It makes you nervous too. And you should be. Something is going on over there that doesn't include ghosts."

His attitude made me angry. "It's been twelve years. It's not like you've been calling and checking up on me. I haven't seen or heard from you through a lot of serious things that have happened in my life. It's too late to want to protect me now. I can take care of myself."

Daniel put his hands on my arms, his face close to mine. "It's not the same, Lisa. This is murder. I don't want you to die. I'm sorry we fell out of touch. I thought that was what you wanted. You made it pretty clear that you didn't want to see me."

My mind immediately wandered back to the last time I'd seen him before our meeting at Simon's house. It wasn't a passionately charged goodbye, but I conceded that both our feelings had been raw at the time.

"I never said that." I wasn't sure exactly what I'd said—I knew my mother had been listening in the next room. "I don't want to die either, but I think you're making more of this than there is. Believe me, I'm perfectly safe."

"You'll have to forgive me if I want to be sure of that." He opened the car door for me. "I'll be around until this is over."

I got in the car and locked the doors after he closed mine. He didn't leave Barry's house until I pulled out onto the road. I knew he followed me home. I was confused about how to take his new concern for my safety. I knew it would only last until he decided if Ashcroft was behind Simon's poisoning. And that was okay. Maybe Daniel was right, and Ashcroft would be willing to kill me to get back at his father. It wouldn't help him get the house when something happened to Simon, but maybe it was the revenge factor.

Knowing something like that could be real, I parked the Beetle and quickly went into the house. The lights from Daniel's car went off when I was inside, but his car stayed at the curb. I was kind of flattered that he cared enough to stake out the place. Then I reminded myself that he might do it for anyone and it was nothing personal.

Simon was asleep with Puck lying on top of him. They were both snoring. Wordsworth looked up with one eye open when I went into his room. Maggie May and Truffles followed me, as silent as the darkness from one room to another.

But Dickens was waiting to ambush me on the circular stairs. "You're finally returned. I've been pondering what you said about other writers trying to complete my work. It is obvious to me that my ending for Edward Drood must be absolutely different that anything they could dream up. And to that end, I am ready for you to continue my story."

"I'm really tired." I slowly climbed the stairs. "Maybe tomorrow night."

"Nonsense. There is no time like the present. I find you make too many excuses as to why your writing and other tasks aren't completed. You must mentally prepare yourself if you want your life to be successful. Up and to the *computer*, as you say. I am ready to dictate my tale to you."

I yawned. "All right. We can work for a while. You know you could do some of this by yourself. You managed to move things. You could move a pen across the paper."

He met me again at the top of the stairs going into my room. "Why would I waste my energy on such a task when I have you?"

We began working, Dickens moving back and forth through the room as he dictated. I envied his ease with words, especially after two hundred years. I had trouble going back to my story after not working on it for a few days.

His voice was powerful and yet subtle. He didn't knock me down with the ideas, and yet I understood clearly what was going on. Despite myself, it was a pleasure helping him work. He truly was a master storyteller. I hoped one day to be as good.

I stretched my shoulders and rubbed my eyes as he paused to consider a story point that he was unsure on. I glanced at the time on the computer and couldn't believe four hours had gone by.

"Sorry. It's after two. I have to get some sleep." I yawned. "Great storytelling."

His face took on a twisted expression. "But I have more to say. We aren't finished."

I got up from the computer and stretched again. "That's all I can do today. We'll work on it again tomorrow, if you like."

"Wait."

"Really. You're a workhorse, that's for sure but—"

"No, you ninny. Be silent. Something is amiss in the house. Don't you hear it?"

I listened. "No. I don't hear anything."

But a shiver of fear slipped through me after Daniel's warning. I went to the window and look down into the street. His car was still there.

"Wordsworth would've barked if he heard anything."

"That puny pup. He's a sorry excuse for a watchdog."

"Hey, there's no reason to badmouth him. He's just a puppy."

He stopped again and actually put a hand to his ear. "I tell you, something is not right. You should alert Canterville. Turn on the lights. Call the servants to hand."

Smiling, I started to get in bed. "I'm going to sleep. There are no servants. And I don't hear anything unusual."

Maggie May and Truffles were both on the bed already, stretching and making room when they saw me come toward the bed. I didn't know what was wrong with Dickens. Maybe this was his way of getting me to go back to work. It wasn't going to happen. My eyes ached for sleep.

And then I heard a noise too. I couldn't tell what it was. Probably nothing. It sounded like someone dragging a chair or some piece of furniture across a floor, with no interest in whether or not they were damaging the floor.

"You hear it," Dickens said. "I believe someone has breached your security."

"No way. No one could get in with the system locked. It can't happen."

There was a thud that sounded as though it came from the second floor.

"What say you now?"

I gulped hard. "I say go check it out."

"Excuse me?" He looked offended. "I am not your

servant."

"No, but you're a ghost, and you can't get hurt. You could go down there and see if something is really wrong. I hate to call Daniel if it's just Puck playing with books. Go look at it."

He raised his chin and stared away from me. "I shall not. You must develop your own courage, Miss Wellman. Perhaps if you do, writing will not come so hard to you. A writer must be courageous, willing to set his sail away from the shore."

"Fine. But if I get killed, who will you coerce into writing the rest of your book?" I got off the bed, grabbed the flashlight from the bedside table, and left the bedroom.

There was a secret door in what had become the Jules Verne room because it was filled with science fiction. Simon had shown it to me as we walked through the house the first time. The door opened from behind a panel in the wall that was accessed by the twist of an angel's head in the carved fireplace hearth. It opened to a small landing and a staircase that led to the second floor into the Teddy Roosevelt room, which housed historical fiction.

I carefully and quietly opened the secret door and followed the staircase. It was dark, hence the flashlight, which I doused as soon as I got to the second floor. I listened for a moment but didn't hear anything else. I hoped it was safe to go out and that it was only another ghost or something. Taking my courage that had been questioned by Dickens in hand, I pushed open the door and stepped into the room.

There was nothing to see here. I waited until I heard another thumping and scraping sound. It definitely wasn't Puck, as much as I wanted it to be. I realized that I'd left my cell phone in my bedroom and hoped I didn't need it until I had a chance to go back upstairs. I didn't want to call anyone until I knew if this was actually a threat. The only way to find out was to stumble into whatever it was.

Since the Teddy Roosevelt room was empty, I felt my way down the dark hall to the Jane Austen room, which held our romance collection. My eyes were used to the dark by then. No one was in that room either.

Okay. On to the Lewis Carroll room for children's books.

We'd put some antique toys in the room—a rocking horse, some dolls, and a few large, wooden soldiers. Personally, the dolls creeped me out, but Simon loved them sitting in the room in tiny chairs. I tried not to focus on them as my eyes swept the room. No one else was there.

Except the dolls with their weird eyes and tiny teeth.

I'd been much too involved in the paranormal recently.

There was one more room on this floor. It was the James Michener room for adventure, fiction and nonfiction. I'd been sure the sound had come from the second floor, but I might have been wrong. It seemed too loud to come from the ground floor. The only way to find out was to check it out.

And there was where I found our unwelcome intruder. A lantern-shaped flashlight picked him out. He was piling books in the middle of the floor. A red gas can was beside him, the smell of fumes from it already strong. I had no doubt there were matches or a lighter ready to be used.

I was horrified.

I switched on the overhead light and called out, "What the heck do you think you're doing?"

Chapter Twenty-two

The Reveal

"Have a heart that never hardens."

It was Ashcroft.

I couldn't believe he wanted to set the house on fire. I hoped at this late juncture that he didn't also have a gun—possibly the French dueling pistol that he'd used to shoot Mr. Hart so he could blame the death on his father. My mind leapt from one conclusion to the next. I wasn't prepared for this, but when is the heroine ever ready to confront the bad guy?

"You," he accused. "This is all your fault. My father would never have gone through with this stupid idea to make the house a book shop if you wouldn't have encouraged him. He's talked about it since my mother died. All I had to do was wait, and he'd have forgotten about it. The house would've been mine."

"The house can still be yours. I don't want it. I didn't know Simon had plans for this. I tried to talk him out of it once I found out. This house should rightfully be yours. Don't destroy it, please. We can work something out."

"I think it's too late for that, Miss Wellman. There's only one thing left to do." He took out a match—I knew it had to be there somewhere—and struck it. He held it dramatically above the books for a moment. "Goodbye."

As the match dropped from his fingers, I moved toward the heavy drapes at the large window that overlooked the backyard. Without hesitation, I ripped them down and turned to smother the flames with them.

Ashcroft hadn't had a chance to throw gasoline on the books, but they were beginning to burn, even without the accelerant. He reached for the gas can when he saw me rushing toward him, probably looking like a mad woman bent on devastation. Appropriately, he gasped and ran, leaving the gas can in the room beside the fire.

I didn't even think of chasing him. My mind was focused on only one thing—saving the books. I would always be a librarian. My preservation instincts came out as I threw the drapes on the fire and began batting it out. My hands felt hot after a few minutes, but I didn't stop to look at them until the smoke alarm went off.

The house alarm began screaming too. Wordsworth heard it and came running as fast as his little legs would carry him. Puck skidded into the room right after him.

The fire was out, but the room was filled with smoke. I started coughing and sat down on the floor to take a look at the damage. I prayed it wasn't too bad.

That was where Daniel found me after pounding on the door didn't work and he kicked it open. That was going to be expensive to repair. The sound of sirens came quickly on his heels, but by that time, he'd already picked me up and taken me outside into the chilly night air.

"Are you okay?" He pushed my hair out of my face. "What were you doing? Was it candles with the ghost or something?"

"No." My voice was hoarse, and I could barely speak for coughing. "It was Ashcroft. He was going to set the house on fire. I bet he poisoned Simon too."

Two fire trucks and an ambulance arrived. Despite Daniel's protesting, I grabbed the arm of the first firefighter as he headed toward the broken front door. "It's only some smoke now on the second floor. No equipment, please. Enough damage has been done already. We have thousands of books inside. No water."

I told him about Simon being in the basement and admitted I wasn't sure where the three cats and Wordsworth were located, even as I saw Puck run out the front door.

The firefighter acknowledged my request with a curt nod, but he still walked into the house with an axe. I ran after him, screaming, but Daniel pulled me back and held me in his arms until a paramedic arrived to tell me I needed oxygen. I was crying so hard that I could barely catch my breath, but there was nothing more I could do.

"This is the ghost house that was on TV," another fireman said to his comrade as they walked inside past me. "You think the ghost set it on fire?"

I couldn't pay attention to anything after that. I sat on the ground with the paramedic holding the oxygen mask against my face. Daniel had gone inside and came back with Maggie May and Truffles. He put them in his car, which was thoughtful of him, as they were still acclimating to the change in residence. They could have gotten lost.

Two firefighters walked Simon out of the house a moment later. He was wearing his pajamas with the British flag splayed across them. He seemed confused and upset, as anyone would, but otherwise he was fine.

"Are you all right, Miss Wellman?" he inquired. "This is a hellish experience. What on earth happened?"

I told him. It broke my heart to see him try to hold back his tears. His lip trembled, but he kept his chin up and stiff. "I'm so sorry. I feel terrible about what happened. I wish you would change your will and give the house to Ashcroft. It really does belong to him, Simon."

"You are a far better person than I, Elizabeth Wellman. Where did the miscreant run to? A stern talking to is required. His mother and I were too soft on the boy and apparently didn't impress the importance of life on him." He waved away the offer of an oxygen mask and a blanket.

"I don't know where he is. He ran off as I was trying to put out the flames. I don't know how many books were ruined, but at least the house was saved."

He put one arm around me. "You are a brave woman, a heroine worthy of any novel. It is a pleasure to know you."

Daniel came around the side of the house with Ashcroft. He already had him in handcuffs. They were both covered in dirt as though they'd rolled on the ground. Two police cars edged as close to the curb as they could. He handed Simon's son off to them and came to check on us.

"Everything okay here?" he asked as he crouched close to us.

"Yes. Thank you."

"I'm sorry I didn't realize what was going on until the alarm sounded. How did he get inside?"

"I fear that was my doing, sir," Simon replied. "He is my son, and as such, I believed he needed the security code Miss Wellman had devised. I apologize. Ashcroft is obviously disturbed and must have proper help."

"There was no way you could know what he'd do, Mr. Canterville. He was right behind the house, waiting to see it on fire. Most people who light things up want to see the flames. I think you prevented that, Lisa."

He reached out and took one of my hands. My quick yelp told us both that something was wrong.

"Your hands," he said. "You're burned. Didn't you notice?"

I hadn't, but I did then. Both my hands felt as though they were actually on fire. Knowing something about burns from a three-day seminar for writers put on by local firefighters, I knew that was a good sign. They were burned but not as badly as they might have been.

Daniel called the paramedic back again, and they insisted on taking me to the hospital. I wasn't in any shape to disagree, but I was glad to see one of the firefighters hand Wordsworth to Simon as I walked to the ambulance. Now all we had to do was coax Puck back into the house again. At least everyone was okay.

Simon was persuaded to accompany me, even though he insisted that he was fine. Daniel promised to take care of Wordsworth, Maggie May, and Truffles until we got back. I could hear the firefighters discussing that there was nothing for them to do. They'd confiscated the gas can for evidence, but not a single axe had gone through a door, wall, or bookcase. Not a single drop of water had been used. I had done an adequate job.

With that knowledge, I lay back against the stretcher and passed out.

* * *

When I woke up I was in the emergency room, my hands had been bandaged—lucky it was only the palms so I could still type and shelve books.

"There you are." Simon was sitting beside me. "Is there someone I can call for you? I believe you mentioned that you have two sisters. Would you like me to phone them?"

"No, thanks. They'd just make a fuss, and it's not really that bad. How are you doing?"

"I'm fine, my dear. Disappointed in myself as a father but otherwise well." His lean face looked more haggard than usual. This happening on top of the poisoning was difficult.

"Well, let's get out of here. I want to see if there are books that need to be replaced. Also if there is any smoke damage to the James Michener room. Where's Daniel? He's our best bet of getting a quick ride home."

"I haven't seen him, but he did say he would keep an eye on the rest of the family. Perhaps he was called to work."

I realized that I didn't have my handbag with me and didn't know his cell number. I supposed I could have called him at work but felt bad about doing it. "Let's just get a taxi."

"Unfortunately, I didn't have time to bring my wallet. Do you have any cash, Miss Wellman?"

"No, but surely a driver would wait until one of us could run in and get some money."

"Admirable idea! But you always have them. I agree that we should leave this place. I've seen too much of it in recent days."

What we didn't think about was that the hospital wasn't going to simply let us walk out without some guarantee of payment. Without anything—including ID—we had to wait there while Bob Stanhope came to rescue us.

A doctor came in and told me what I should do for my hands over the next week or two. He gave me some bandages and ointment to use on them. He said the burns weren't too bad and over the counter medication should take care of any pain. I thanked him and got my things together.

I wasn't sure how long we waited before Bob finally arrived. He was upset about the house and Ashcroft. "Do you want me to represent him, Simon?

Or should I find someone who can handle a capital case?"

"Why would this be a felony?" I asked while we waited for the hospital to come up with a bill for their services."

"Setting fire to a house is a felony," he calmly recited. "And that's not to say that he may have killed Ebenezer Hart. I'm not sure I would be qualified to take that kind of case to court."

"Yes," Simon replied. "I don't plan to press charges against my son, and naturally I want him to have the best representation."

"Of course." Bob nodded.

"But why assume Ashcroft also killed Mr. Hart?" I wondered. "The two may have nothing to do with one another."

Bob scrutinized me as though I was a small, possibly mentally deficient child. "My goodness, Miss Wellman. I would hope the two events were the responsibility of one man. I would hate to think there was more than one person who would do such a thing to Mr. Canterville. Wouldn't you?"

Simon paid for everything—generous of him. I didn't argue the point with Bob. He might have been right. It would make more sense than someone poisoning Simon and someone else killing Mr. Hart and leaving him to be found on the roof.

Although why Ashcroft would have killed Mr. Hart to keep Simon from giving me the house was difficult to understand.

Still the vagaries of the human mind were much more difficult to understand than poison, guns, and fire. I decided to wait to see what Daniel learned and go from there.

The fire department was still at the house when we got back. A man at the door told us we would have to wait outside until their investigation was complete. I'd forgotten that the house had become a crime scene inside and outside now. It was inconvenient.

"Let's get a late breakfast, shall we?" Simon offered me his arm. "Perhaps these men will be finished when we return."

The man at the door waved to Bob, who had driven us home and waited to see what we wanted to do. But Bob either ignored him or didn't see. "I could drive you wherever you want."

"I appreciate that," Simon said. "But the Bentley is up and running. We aren't forced to take Miss Wellman's vehicle. I should enjoy driving us to the coffee shop after I sneak in through the basement and fetch my wallet."

"I'm a mess," I told him. "I don't think I can go out like this. And you're still wearing your pajamas and slippers. I don't think we can sneak in for that long. We'll have to make do here."

"I can get something for you," Bob offered. He was certainly much better in a time of crisis than he was ordinarily.

But Mrs. Tappen had other ideas as she bustled up in a brown power suit accented with orange. "For goodness sake—what you've been through this week. It's terrible. Come to my house. I'll have Cecily make you some eggs and tea. There's no point in arguing with me. This is already decided. Come along now, before they arrest you for getting in the way."

I'd never heard of a charge of getting in the way,

although there was impeding an investigation, which we surely weren't doing. But there was no way out of going to Mrs. Tappen's house.

Bob got off easy, leaving with a promise to find the best lawyer for Ashcroft. I wished I could have gone with him. Considering how I normally felt about him, that said a lot for how I felt about having breakfast with Mrs. Tappen.

The Admiral was already seated in her drawing room with a partial cup of coffee in his hand. "What a tragedy. It's difficult to believe that this world is in such a sorry state. Not enough discipline, Miss Wellman. The same excuse for people wandering the streets in their pajamas."

"We were just rescued from a fire, Admiral Leazer. Of course we aren't dressed like we're going to a party. We're lucky to be alive."

Mrs. Tappen ordered breakfast from Cecily and then joined us at the table. "Yes, but I understand what William is saying. After all, Simon's son—his own flesh and blood—took advantage of knowing that his father was allergic to lavender oil and attempted to poison him with it."

I was surprised to discover that she knew about Simon's allergy. But we already knew Ashcroft had tried to poison him. He'd confessed to it last night. There was no reason to be suspicious of Mrs. Tappen.

Hmm.

Chapter Twenty-three

Don't Look Away

"The beating of my heart was so violent and wild that I felt as though my life were breaking from me."

After runny eggs and slightly burnt toast, Simon and I walked to the house. We were both relieved to see the firetruck was gone. There was a note on the front door thanking us for our cooperation and saying that the investigation was complete. It was taped to the door that was barely on its hinges after Daniel's assault against it.

"Well." Simon smiled at me. "Good news, then. I could use a bit of it after that horrible breakfast. I believe we still need to do some shopping, Miss Wellman, if we are to prevent anything of the sort again. Please remind me that the only thing worse than Mrs. Tappen is her housekeeper's cooking."

I laughed but felt exactly the same. "I'm going to take a shower and change clothes."

"Was I wrong when I thought I heard the doctor say you shouldn't get your hands wet?"

"I don't care. I have smoke in my hair and everywhere else. I'm taking a shower."

"Perhaps we can accommodate the doctor's wishes and yours. Come with me."

Simon tried his best to put plastic gloves on my hands but the bandages were too bulky. He finally put a plastic bag on each hand and taped it closed with duct tape. It was weird but better than no shower.

"You know, something is bothering me about all this," he said as he taped. "I know Ashcroft is upset about the house. But why would he want to kill Mr. Hart?"

"I've been thinking the same thing." I flexed my hands inside the bags. "The most he could gain would be you as a suspect in Mr. Hart's death. And that was easily explained. Even the French dueling pistol wasn't much evidence against you."

He sighed. "I suppose we must assume that Ashcroft hatched the plot to poison me when he realized he'd killed a man for no reason. It pains me to think that, and perhaps that is why it bothers me. Still, I feel I should mention it to his lawyer. He may be guilty of arson and poisoning but not murder."

"You could be right. I hope so. I'm not sure. I don't think he wanted to kill us by starting the fire. Killing someone is different, right? We don't know that he wouldn't have come to his senses at the last minute and gotten us out of the house in time."

"Thank you for trying to make me feel better, but your poor hands are a reminder of the fact that he'd already set the fire. If you hadn't acted, we would both be dead. I love my son. I hope there is some help for him."

We parted ways in the foyer. Simon went to his room to call about having the front door repaired and telling Bob that he didn't think his son had killed Mr. Hart. After that, we were going to look at the damage done to the James Michener room.

The shower was tricky—try turning faucets with your bandaged hands in plastic bags—but I made it work, and it was wonderful. Taking off my clothes hadn't been easy and putting clothes on again was even harder. It was strange to be in the bedroom without Maggie May and Truffles. Once I got dressed I could have Simon call Daniel to let him know we were home and he could bring back my cats and Wordsworth.

"I suppose you'll want to use this as an excuse not to continue my work." Dickens formed in front of me with a belligerent expression on his face.

"Do you mind?"

He suddenly noticed my state of undress and quickly turned the other way. "My apologies. I thought you'd be finished by now."

I held up my burned hands and shrugged. "I think I can still type once I get the baggies off, but dressing is really a problem."

"No doubt. No doubt. Yet you saved the house and most of the books. I was certainly happy to find that my books were unharmed."

There was one button at the neck of my top that I just couldn't take care of with the bags on my hands. Brushing my hair was another problem, but it would have to do.

"You could have helped last night, and possibly no books would have been burned. Were you this cantankerous in life?"

He turned and assumed a self-important air. "I beg your pardon? I was the most beloved author of my time — possibly my century. You know nothing about me."

Someone was pounding on the useless door downstairs.

"Lisa?" It was Daniel yelling for me.

"I have to go. Make yourself scarce. We'll talk later. Maybe I won't add what a useless ghost you were to the end of your book."

"What say you? You would not dare."

"Oh, I'd dare. You should know that about me by now." I grinned as I left him in the bedroom.

Daniel was waiting at the bottom of the stairs. "I was a little worried when I heard you'd left the hospital. You should've called me. I would've come to get you."

"Everything was here after our mad dash out last night, including my cell phone and the business card with your number on it. But Simon called his lawyer. We were fine."

"What's this?" He looked at my hands.

My face got hot as he stared at them. Darn burned hands and plastic bags. "I wanted to take a shower. Simon came up with this idea. But now I can't get them off to work the buttons."

He could have helped me with the tape and plastic bags first. Instead he buttoned my top buttons and flicked a lock of hair out of my face. "I'm sorry you got burned. You shouldn't have tried to take care of it yourself. I guess I should have camped out in here instead of staying outside. It feels like I'm always letting you down."

I was caught between crying and throwing my arms around his neck. It was just as well that my hands were in baggies.

"I talked to Ashcroft last night." He slowly removed the duct tape and baggies from my hands. "He admits to poisoning his father, though he claims he knew it wasn't enough lavender to kill him, just make him sick."

"Not sure how he knew that. I took a course in poisons, and I think it would be difficult to gauge the amount since Simon is also allergic to it."

"He also claims that he didn't intend to hurt you or Simon last night. He planned to wake you up and get you out of the house after he started the fire."

I took the soggy bags and tape from him. "That was a long shot. Do you believe him?"

"It's hard to say. I've heard people say crazier things." He looked at me on the stair above him. "But he swears he didn't kill Ebenezer Hart. I've talked to the other detectives on the case, and they can't figure out why he'd kill him either. His motive doesn't make any sense."

"But you've seen people with less motive go to jail, right?"

"Yes. Everyone, including the DA, wants to charge

him with the murder. He had access to the house and the dueling pistol. He could have thought framing Simon for his murder would be enough to make him reconsider the book shop. When he found out that wasn't the case, he went to more extreme measures."

"You don't believe it, do you?" I searched his eyes. "You think someone else killed Mr. Hart."

"I do. I don't know who, and I don't know if I'm going to have a chance to explore it. Chief Masterson wants the case closed and wants me to get back to my regular duties."

"I guess that's what you'll have to do. Even if the wrong person goes to prison."

"It's a long time until that happens. Maybe whoever killed Mr. Hart will show his hand before then. It's a long shot, but it's all we've got."

We went down the stairs. "I was about to call you and ask if you could bring Maggie May, Wordsworth, and Truffles home."

"They're staying with a friend of mine who's a veterinarian. We can get them anytime you're ready."

"Great. Thanks for taking such good care of them. Let me tell Simon. We were about to look at the Michener room and then go shopping, but I know he'll want to do this first. I thought he'd be up here by now. I'll be right back."

"Good. Maybe I'll see your famous ghost while I'm waiting."

"Not if you're lucky. Dickens was a good writer, but he has a demanding personality."

I heard scratching at the back door and glanced carefully out the window. It was Puck. I was thrilled to see him there. It's hard to tell with a wild cat if they'll take to you or not. Since he came back after running out, I guessed that meant he was back for good. I made sure there was food in his bowl and opened the kitchen door.

"Come on. You know you want to."

He looked up at me and meowed before swishing his tail and running into the house, straight to the food bowl. I didn't try to stroke him right away. Sometimes that put him off. Instead I told him how happy I was to see him. He glanced at me and meowed again as though saying, *me too.*

I opened the door to the basement and called Simon's name. He didn't respond, and I had a moment of dread that I attributed to finding him after Ashcroft had poisoned him. That was silly, of course, since Ashcroft was in jail and couldn't hurt anyone.

"Simon? Daniel's here. I thought we might get the cats and Wordsworth before we go food shopping. Are you dressed?"

Still no response. I felt cold all over, and my hands hurt. I silently prayed that he hadn't hurt himself or had some new reaction to what he'd been through. Then I pushed my reluctant legs and feet down the rest of the stairs.

"Simon?" The lights were on, and he'd laid out clean clothes on the bed. But otherwise there was no sign of him.

"Daniel!" I yelled. "Something has happened to Simon."

Chapter Twenty-four

Wherefore Art Thou?

"I have known a vast quantity of nonsense talked about bad men."

We looked everywhere through the house and outside in the yard. I called the Admiral and Mrs. Tappen, but neither of them had seen Simon.

"Where could he have gone?" I asked Daniel, even though I knew he had no idea either. "He couldn't just disappear."

He took out his phone. "I'm calling in a Silver Alert for him. You haven't known him long enough to know if he has spells where he wanders off. Sometimes people do that. Or it could be due to everything he's been through in the last few days. Either way, he needs help."

As he set things up with the police, I looked through Simon's belongings to see if there was any clue as to what his mindset was when he'd left. Maybe he was hungry. He knew there was no food here and went out to get some without saying anything. But in his pajamas? That seemed unlikely.

I found one of his slippers near the basement door going outside. Surely he wouldn't have gone out with one shoe on. I opened the door and went outside. Because there was still light frost on the ground, I noticed his footsteps—one shoe—one bare foot. I followed that track until it ended at the driveway. It wasn't a careful path. At one point it twisted around, and there was a red plastic button. I was sure it was from his pajamas.

Hurrying back inside, I grabbed Daniel and showed him what I'd found.

"Good job, Sherlock." He crouched beside the button and unusual footsteps. "You should give up working with books and come to work for the police. It looks like Simon might have been abducted."

"It was as we feared," I said solemnly. "Mr. Hart's killer has returned to kidnap him."

"That sounds a little iffy."

"Maybe. But can you think of a better reason for Simon to have disappeared? The killer was worried that Simon realized who he is."

"Let's put that idea on the back burner for now. The important thing is to find him."

Dozens of police and volunteers came to the house

for pictures of Simon to help find him. I made copies of a picture I found and distributed it to everyone who asked. Daniel coordinated their efforts with a map of Olde Town. Everyone spread through the area to cover as much space as possible.

"Still," I said to Dickens as we watched the group disperse from the front yard. "It's like looking for a needle in a haystack. He could be anywhere."

"So true, though your populace does you credit by turning out in such numbers to search for him."

"I wish I understood why he was taken. If I could get into the killer's mind, it would make the search go faster."

"Doubtless you have till nightfall. If Canterville isn't immediately dispatched, the killer will wait until it is dark."

"That's probably true." I sat at the rosewood dining table and tried to think why the killer would take Simon now. "It has to be that something happened that made him think Simon suspected him. If so, it might have something to do with Ashcroft. Maybe something about Ashcroft's arrest made Simon realize that he wasn't the killer but he knew who was."

"Perhaps. And perhaps Canterville, without thinking, alerted the killer to his knowledge. Who has he spoken to about this?"

Daniel had asked me to stay at the house in case Simon returned. It was the worst job for a worried mind. I wanted to be out on the streets, pounding on doors and demanding to search houses.

"Okay." I found a piece of paper and a pencil. "One of the seminars on police psychology said that police officers take notes so they can put the events together and find the perp."

"Perp?" Dickens frowned. "Is that a modern name for killer?"

"It means perpetrator. Someone who did the crime, no matter what crime. Now let's think about who Simon spoke to about this in the past few days. Definitely me. We talked about it with the Admiral and Mrs. Tappen—I've considered her being guilty of poisoning Simon because she secretly didn't want us to open the book shop next door to her. But since Ashcroft admitted that he did it, I don't think she was capable of killing and placing Mr. Hart's body on the roof."

"A nice touch, that," Dickens admired. "I should have liked to have killed someone in a novel that way."

"But let's face it. It took someone strong, even if they were in the house and put him on the roof from my window. Mrs. Tappen couldn't have lifted Mr. Hart."

He put one hand on his hip as he began pacing back and forth though the air. "Then we must assume a gentleman is responsible. He must be in robust health and of a sturdy constitution. What of the Admiral? Is he capable?"

"I'm not sure. He could be stronger than he appears." I considered Admiral Leazer. It was hard to tell. Just because he was older didn't make him too weak to be counted as a possible killer. "We did just speak with him this morning. Maybe one of us said something that made him believe we suspected him. And he does live right next door, so it would be easy to grab him."

"There must be a test of his strength. If accused, he would certainly deny his involvement."

"What kind of test?"

"Perhaps you could hurl something at him, something extremely heavy. If he catches it, you would know he is your culprit."

"But if it was something that weighed as much as Mr. Hart, I couldn't pick it up to hurl it at him."

He put a hand to his chin, one almost blending into the other. "Quite so. Perhaps your lover might be up to the task."

"If you're talking about Daniel, he's not my lover. He could probably pick up something big enough to test the Admiral, but what reason would I give him?"

"You're a woman, my dear. The fairer sex has no rhyme or reason. Just ask him to do it. No doubt he will, solely to impress you and lure you back to his bed."

"It doesn't work that way now. I'm not sure it ever did." I saw Daniel coming up the walk.

"Are you questioning my grasp on human nature? I tell you now, my girl. No man who looks at a female the way he looks at you will deny you."

Daniel came in and glanced around the front parlor. "I thought I heard you talking to someone. I hoped Simon was back."

"No." Dickens hadn't moved, but Daniel couldn't see him. "I was just muttering, trying to make some sense of things. Do you think Admiral Leazer could be responsible for Mr. Hart's death and Simon's disappearance?"

"I don't know. Have you had some insight or something you remembered? I suppose living right next door would be handy."

"I'm just not sure he would be strong enough to

put Mr. Hart on the roof. And that's the only thing that makes sense."

"Maybe. Let's go ask him and take a look in his house while we're there."

"You think he'll just let you go in and look around?"

Daniel shrugged. "If he's not guilty of anything."

"Okay. Let's go."

We went next door. The Admiral was walking his fox terrier in the front yard. He didn't look welcoming when he saw us coming toward him. Daniel smiled and nodded to him. "Good morning, sir. We met the day you called in about the dead man on the roof next door. I'm Deputy Chief Daniel Fairhaven."

"Of course. I remember you. What can I do for you now?"

"We're looking for Mr. Canterville, sir. He may have wandered away from the house. Have you seen him?"

"I haven't seen him, or I would have sent him home."

"Would you mind if we take a look inside in case he slipped in somehow? I'm not accusing you of anything. Just trying to look everywhere we can."

The Admiral's expression stiffened. I thought he'd say no. Then he surprised me by his answer. "Whatever you need to find the poor man."

"Thank you, sir." Daniel nodded to him, and we left him there with his dog.

"I guess that means he's not guilty," I whispered as we walked away.

"Let's take a quick look inside, just in case." Daniel winked at me. "You never know."

But even though we looked everywhere in the Admiral's house, there was no sign of Simon. I thought about the test Dickens had proposed, but really this one was better. I had to go back to the possible suspect list to reconsider who the killer could be.

"What are you doing?" Daniel asked when he saw my piece of paper.

"Trying to decide which of the possible suspects killed Mr. Hart and now has Simon."

"And who do you think is a possible suspect?"

"Anyone Simon spoke to yesterday or today." I crossed the Admiral off the list. "He talked to you, but we'll assume you're not the killer."

"Thanks. Who else?"

"I don't know." I rubbed my forehead, starting to get a headache. "Bob Stanhope, Simon's lawyer, I guess. He knew everything, including that Simon wanted to give me the house because he felt like Ashcroft wouldn't take care of it."

And then it hit me.

"It has to be Bob Stanhope. He and Simon discussed giving me the house two weeks ago. It appeared that Ashcroft just found out yesterday when Bob was here, but he told me when he tried to torch the house that he poisoned Simon when he found out. That was the day before. The only person who knew then was Bob. He has to be the killer."

Daniel closed his eyes and opened them. "Your logic is making me dizzy. Even if Bob told Ashcroft that he was about to lose his inheritance, that doesn't make Bob the killer. The two don't even go together."

"Simon was planning to call Bob this morning. He didn't say what for, but he told me that he was suspicious of someone. It could have been Bob, and he gave himself away when he was talking to him. So Bob decided to kidnap and kill Simon."

"Even if that's true, and I'm certainly not saying it is — what motive does Bob Stanhope have for killing Ebenezer Hart? Whether or not Simon could build his book shop here wouldn't impact his lawyer."

I nibbled on my thumbnail as I stalked back and forth across the room in front of Dickens. He seemed to be pondering the issue too. "We'll just have to find a way to prove it. I know in my gut that this is right. What does your gut tell you?"

"My gut, which admittedly is heavily influenced by my sister being the DA, tells me that we don't have a case against Bob Stanhope and what we have probably isn't even enough to get a search warrant for his house to look for Simon."

His phone rang, and he walked away to answer it. I stared at the back of his coat for a moment. I knew I was right about this. It wasn't just that Bob told Ashcroft about Simon setting me in his will to inherit the house. There was more to it than that. I just had to figure out what.

"We just had a sighting of an older person wandering around on First Street. It could be Simon. I'll check it out. Don't worry about who killed Mr. Hart right now. Let's focus on getting Simon back home. Okay?"

"Sure."

"I'll call you either way." He hugged me. "It's going to be okay, Lisa."

The hug threw me off. I wasn't able to come up with a snappy retort until he was already going out the door. "But what if Simon is gone because Bob killed Mr. Hart? What about that?"

"Too late, my dear," Dickens said. "But your theory seems valid to me. You must focus on proving it to your lover."

"He's not my lover. He's just affectionate during times of stress." I ran upstairs. "The best way to prove this is to look up Mr. Hart and Bob Stanhope on the computer. I'll bet we find something."

Dickens was at the top of each flight of stairs. "Why waste valuable time when you could be finishing my story?"

"I'm not working on my story or yours until Simon is safely home. You better get used to that idea."

Chapter Twenty-five

The Answer is Simple

"The world lay spread before me."

I put both men's names into Google. It seemed I was right and they not only worked together as lawyers some years back but had business dealings today.

"Bob and Ebenezer were working on a waterfront property development that could be worth millions." I sat back and considered everything that had happened. "What if Bob decided he wanted the whole pie, not just a piece of it?"

"Even in my day, killing his partner would be an

excellent way to take advantage of that opportunity."

"And Ebenezer's feud with Simon made this a great opportunity. He could get rid of his partner and blame it on Simon by putting his corpse on our roof after shooting him with Simon's dueling pistol — which Bob had access to. He had keys to the house and could have put Ebenezer on the roof while we were gone that night. He was strong enough to drag him to my window and throw him out."

"Yes! That seems to be the plot." He frowned. "But how to prove it? How did Simon deduce the problem?"

"Simon was suspicious about Ashcroft being blamed for the attacks against him and killing Mr. Hart. He probably said something he shouldn't when he called Bob."

My phone rang. It was much harder to push the buttons on it than it was to use the computer with my palms bandaged. "Yes?"

"I'm sorry, Lisa," Daniel said. "It wasn't Simon. I'm coming back to your place. Don't do anything without me, okay?"

"Thanks. I won't. See you in a few." I pushed the off button. "There's only one way to get to the heart of this," I said to Dickens. "I have to confront Bob before it's too late. There's no reason for him to wait to kill Simon. He's already killed once."

"Best to hurry, then. I don't believe the man you prefer not to call your lover will want to take part. There are times one must advance alone."

"You're right. I think this might be one of those times. Thanks for your help."

"Bear that in mind upon your return, as I shall have need of your services."

I wished I had some kind of weapon, but then realized I was better off not allowing things to get to that point. I had to be clever, I told myself as I checked my GPS for Bob's home. I had to be smarter.

"And crazy for doing this." I started the Beetle and pulled out of the driveway around the Bentley.

Bob lived outside Olde Town. I followed the GPS until I reached his older, antebellum-type home. It was big, square, and conventionally white, with columns at the front.

He always drove the same black Cadillac. It wasn't parked in the drive. I hoped that meant he wasn't there. A new plan — one in which I saved Simon's life first and then went on to accuse Bob of murder — took form in my mind. I parked the Beetle on the street just before the house. It had been buried in the garage for so long that maybe Bob wouldn't recognize it if he came home.

Speed and timing were of the utmost importance. I sneaked up to the house, watching over my shoulder. I had to search but finally came up with the small lock picking set I kept in my handbag. I'd bought it after a seminar with a private detective who'd shown all the writers how to break into almost everything.

One last scan of the yard and I started opening the lock on the front door. I was having some trouble with it when the door suddenly swung open.

"Yes? Is there something I can do for you?" The woman didn't appear welcoming.

I sucked in a deep breath. *Isabelle Hart*. I knew her from the times I'd gone to court with Simon. This was the last piece of the puzzle. Not only did Bob want all the money from the project he was stealing from Mr. Hart, he also coveted his wife.

Lucky for me that she didn't know who I was.

She frowned carefully, not straining her carefully made-up face. "Wait. I know you. You're Simon Canterville's girl. I saw you in court and in the newspaper. What do you want?"

I took umbrage at being called a girl, but that would have to wait until a time I wasn't worried about anyone dying.

"I'm sorry. Wrong address. Thanks anyway." I started to leave the way I'd come, but Mrs. Hart took out a small pistol and pointed it at my chest — the part of the anatomy I'd learned was easiest to hit. I guess she knew too.

"Stay where you are. Bob?" she called out. "We have another guest."

My heart leapt with joy knowing that the other guest was no doubt Simon. I hoped he was still alive. Then it plummeted when I realized that we were both in jeopardy. I should have gone around back.

Note to self: never have your plucky protagonist approach from the front.

Bob greeted me with a wide smile. "Simon has been longing for company. I think this should be perfect."

"You know the police are right behind me. I just got here a little before them. Did I mention that Deputy Police Chief Daniel Fairhaven is my ex-husband? We're still very tight. Why don't you let Simon go, and we'll leave. We can just forget about all this. No reason to bother the police."

"I thought they were right behind you," Isabelle Hart said in a hateful, suspicious voice.

"Just giving you some options."

Bob grabbed me and jerked me into the house while Isabelle closed and locked the door. She also snatched my cell phone. I couldn't even hope to call Daniel.

"I'll take her downstairs with Simon," he told her. "You get everything together just in case she's telling the truth. It'll only take me a minute to get rid of them. Then we can get out of here."

"What about the money from the project that you murdered Mr. Hart for?" I demanded.

"That's already in my bank in the Caymans." He was nothing if not boastful. "Don't worry, Miss Wellman. We'll be long gone before the police find you. I'm sure Simon has provided funeral benefits for you."

If I let him take me to the basement, Simon and I were both dead. It seemed to me that my odds were better if I let him shoot me while we were struggling for the gun. I had a better chance that he wasn't much of a marksman and he wouldn't kill me. I could get the gun from him and then call Daniel. I liked that plan better and started thinking about which part of my body would be less dangerous for him to shoot.

But as we walked down a long hall, the lights in the house flickered. The landscape art on the walls spun slowly without falling to the floor. There was a nice antique grandfather clock whose hands now moved backwards.

"What's going on?" he asked. "What are you doing?"

"Nothing. How could I even do these things? It looks like your house is haunted too. Maybe you should leave now before something really bad happens."

"Like what? You can't trick me."

The ornate, gilded mirror on the wall trembled as we neared it and then crashed to the floor.

Bob stopped abruptly. "How are you doing this? Stop it right now."

I grinned, sure that Dickens had found some way to escape the confines of the old Victorian. "Don't look now, but he's mad. You won't get away with this."

He pushed the gun to my temple and sneered. "No pitiful attempt at trying to prove my house is haunted is going to stop me, Miss Wellman."

We started past a window that looked out on the front yard. Daniel ran from his car toward the house. Bob's stranglehold on me kept me from pounding on the glass. I couldn't let him know what was happening.

Suddenly Isabelle's scream pierced the house. At the same moment, the window I'd longed to hit shattered, glass flying everywhere. I didn't waste a moment calling out Daniel's name.

At that point, it was as though Bob gave up. He threw me down to the carpeted floor and ran in the direction of Isabelle's calls for help. I continued down the hall at a breakneck pace until I found a door that led to the basement.

"Simon?" I yelled.

"Miss Wellman! Down here."

I started down the stairs to rescue him and hopefully sneak out a back door in case Bob changed his mind about letting me go. I didn't want to risk Daniel taking too long to find us.

There was something—an odd feeling of being watched—a prickling at the back of my neck. I felt cold all over and glanced behind to see if Bob had returned or if Dickens was there with me.

But it wasn't either one.

There will never be a moment in my life that I won't swear that I saw my mother standing at the top of the stairs. She smiled and waved to me before she disappeared. Tears scalded my eyes and ran freely down my face. Was it possible she'd come back to help me?

"Miss Wellman? I assume you are still on your way to release me."

Simon's voice brought me back to the immediate situation. I ran down the rest of the stairs and found him tied to a chair in the damp basement. I got him free, and we hugged before we found the basement door and fled outside into the sunshine.

Chapter Twenty-six

An End to the Tale

"Please, sir. I want some more."

Two weeks later, Simon and I fist bumped as we opened the Canterville Book Shop for business.

It had been a difficult two weeks. The smoke damage was more extensive in the James Michener room than I'd first thought. Many of the books Ashcroft had tried to use to set fire to the house were beyond repair.

It took hours to get the room clean and ready to use. We wouldn't have been able to do it without Dana and her ghost hunters. They said they owed us a favor for putting the house on the news, and I was glad to collect on it.

Daniel had repaired the front door he'd crashed through. It seemed he was into woodwork and carpentry now. We talked about him finding me and Simon that day because I'd mentioned Bob. He swore he wasn't surprised to find I'd gone there without him.

He was surprised, though, to find out that Bob had been a volunteer firefighter in his day. He'd learned how to carry a person over his shoulders, up or down a ladder, and onto the roof—so that's how Ebenezer had gotten up there.

It didn't matter now because everyone was safe. I was still moved to tears every time I thought about seeing my mother that day. I didn't mention it to anyone except Dickens, holding it to myself like a warm hug.

"Why should your mother not have come to save you?" he said as we worked late into the night to finish his final story. "I would have done the same for my daughters, had it been necessary."

That made some kind of sense. I couldn't deny that the spirit world was real since I'd spent every night the last two weeks working with him, after spending all day working on the book shop.

"You know you've never been clear about why you came here," I told him. "What was it? Free secretarial services?"

He put his head back in a manner that I'd come to think of his thinking pose. "Perhaps it was the name of this place matching the name of my own home. Perhaps it was your name—my mother's name was Elizabeth, you know. Or perhaps it was your abysmal writing style that moved me to pity."

"But we haven't really worked on my novel," I reminded him.

"I disagree. Simply working with me on my masterpiece is enough to have taught you something about your own writing. I leave you soon. Continue writing."

Still we managed to make it to opening day. Simon's gigantic, silver-coated cash register rested on the table in the front parlor. Neither one of us could use it, but he said it was good to remind our customers that this was indeed a business establishment. I'd already caught him polishing it several times.

"You have helped me realize my dream, Miss Wellman," Simon said with tears in his pale blue eyes. "Not to mention that you saved my life not once, but twice. I look forward to a long and prosperous partnership with you."

I hugged him. There was no way not to. "I feel exactly the same way. Thank you for offering me this opportunity."

He wiped the tears from his eyes. "I believe that is enough blubbering. Let us welcome our customers."

As soon as the front door was open, Daniel was the first one in the house with a large bouquet of flowers in his hands. Dozens of potential customers came in after him as we moved to the side of the room.

"For luck," he said. "The place looks great. What's next for you, Lisa?"

"Making money at this, I guess. Thanks for the flowers and for everything else."

"Do you think—I mean, this is a long shot—but do you think we could have dinner or something one night? I know we have history, but some of it was good, from what I remember. Maybe we could get to know each other again. You could let me read your book."

"All right." Not like I hadn't considered it as we'd gone through the past few weeks. "I think that would be nice."

I heard laughter from the stairs and knew that Dickens was making fun of me. As Simon commandeered Daniel to show him around the house, I hurried upstairs. Dickens stood in the open window in my room. The wind from the river blew through him but didn't move his clothes or hair.

"Are you leaving?"

"Yes. My time here is done, as is my work, thanks to you. The pain of parting is nothing to the joy of meeting again. One piece of advice I have for you, madam. Never leave anything undone in your life. If you do, it will come back to haunt you."

I watched as he slowly took a step off the window ledge and floated away. Maggie May, Truffles, and Puck watched him from the bed. Wordsworth, still unable to get his tiny legs up the spiral staircase to the third floor, was trying hard to bark on the second floor.

"I guess there's only one thing to say about that: 'It was the best of times, it was the worst of times.'"

British writer Charles Dickens was born on February 7, 1812, in Portsmouth, England. During his writing career he wrote some of the best loved novels of his time—*Oliver Twist, Nicholas Nickleby, David Copperfield, A Tale of Two Cities, Great Expectations*—and *A Christmas Carol*. On June 9, 1870, Dickens died of a stroke in Kent, England, leaving his final novel, *The Mystery of Edwin Drood*, unfinished. His mother's name was Elizabeth.

About the Authors

Joyce and Jim Lavene write award-winning, best-selling mystery and urban fantasy fiction as themselves, J.J. Cook, and Ellie Grant. They have written and published more than 70 novels for Harlequin, Penguin, Amazon, and Simon and Schuster along with hundreds of non-fiction articles for national and regional publications. They live in rural North Carolina with their family, their rescue animals, Quincy - cat, Stan Lee – cat, and Rudi - dog.

Visit them at:
www.joyceandjimlavene.com
www.Facebook.com/JoyceandJimLavene
Amazon Author Central Page:
http://amazon.com/author/jlavene